Lost Snowflakes

Linton Darling

Cover illustration by Nurit Motchan
www.nuronuro.com

This book is written in British English.

*For my snowflake, without whom
I would be lost*

A SURPRISING INVITATION

Like all good books, this is the story of a girl. Some girls are perfect angels, while others are frightful little beasts whom you may find living under toadstools, but Maya Madison was somewhere in between. She was kind and generous, and a fiercely loyal friend who would wrestle twelve tigers to protect those she loved, but when life put the opportunity for pranks, practical jokes or mischief in her path she could rarely resist.

Maya lived with her Aunt Jane and Uncle Bernard in a sleepy little village called Crinkleton. She cared for her aunt and uncle very much but missed her parents, who had been lost while on a scientific expedition to the Arctic when Maya was only three.

Maya went to Crinkleton School with her best friends Jessie and Ella. One crisp autumn day Maya's teacher Miss Acres came to her in the playground and said, "Maya, the Headmaster wants to speak to you in his office please."

Maya's heart sank – it wasn't the first time she had been called into Mr Sneed's office. She hoped she wasn't in trouble. "I've been quite good lately though," she reassured herself as she grabbed a twig from a nearby bush and then followed Miss Acres inside. "Ever since we switched the custard with the mustard in the school kitchen, anyway. I wonder what this is about?"

Mr Sneed was a kindly old man who peered through thick, round glasses, and loved to collect insects. He had lots of unusual books and specimens arranged on his shelves, but Maya tried not to look around her as she knocked on the door and walked into the room, patting her long brown hair into some semblance of order and putting on her most innocent expression. With her small stature, large blue eyes and perfect light dusting of freckles she could look so angelic that many adults found it hard to blame her, however much chaos she might cause. "You wanted to see me, Mr Sneed?" she enquired in her politest voice.

"Ah, young Maya – excellent! Sit down please." The Headmaster showed her to a chair and continued, "Don't worry, you're not here for a telling off this time."

"I have received an email from a school in Siberia called the Taymira Academy. They would like to send one of their best students to our school for two weeks, and for one of our children to go to Siberia in exchange. The girl who is coming here is your age, so I need to choose someone from your class. You are certainly one of our most… erm… creative pupils, so I immediately thought of you. What do you think, would you like to go?"

"Siberia! That's the last thing I expected him to say," thought Maya. "About as likely as nominating me for the 'Best Behaved Student' award or asking to join our street dance group. I'll probably miss my aunt and uncle if I go... but then again, I bet the Siberian school won't give me any homework, and two weeks without homework would be amazing! I'd better not say that though."

"It sounds like it would be an excellent opportunity to enhance my education," she replied, choosing her words carefully, "but I might get a bit lonely. Could I take two of my friends with me?"

"You can as long as their parents agree," Mr Sneed told her, "and of course you will need to get permission from your guardians."

He rose from his chair and turned to look out of the window, at the children in the playground and the village beyond them, nestled amongst the rolling hills of the surrounding countryside. "I'm sure I don't have to tell you Maya, that you will be an ambassador for this school, and must be on your best behaviour. You may find that Taymira is a little stricter than we are here at Crinkleton."

"Yes… best behaviour… very strict," Maya mumbled, as she eased open the lid of a large glass tank on the Headmaster's desk. The tank contained a stick insect she had become rather fond of over the course of several trips to the Head's office. Hating to see any creature imprisoned, Maya had always longed to release "Woody" (as she called him) – and now she saw her chance. As Mr Sneed continued to list the qualities she would need to display in Siberia (good manners, punctuality and obedience), Maya slipped the twig she had brought from the playground into the tank and popped Woody in her pocket.

Just as she had carefully replaced the lid, the Headmaster span around. "In conclusion, Maya: I know I can count on you to be a fine representative of our school. Ah, I see you are admiring my stick insect… he's a fine creature, isn't he?"

"Yes, a real beauty, incredibly stick-like," Maya agreed.

She told the Head she would speak to her aunt and uncle about the trip and decide by the next morning, then made a hasty departure from the office. As she walked back outside her thoughts were racing. An adventure to the other side of the world, with Jessie and Ella! What could be more fun?

KATIA

As soon as she got home that afternoon and had found a place for Woody in her back garden, Maya told Aunt Jane about her conversation with the Headmaster. "He wants me to visit a school in another country for two weeks," she explained.

"I don't know Maya," her aunt replied thoughtfully. "You are very young to spend such a long time away from home. Where exactly is this school?"

"It's in Siberia!"

Aunt Jane looked surprised for a moment. Then she asked Maya to go and play, and had a long conversation on her phone with Uncle Bernard. Afterwards she came up to Maya's little bedroom and said, "We've decided that if you really want to go to Siberia then you can."

"Oh, thank you Auntie!" Maya cried in delight and ran to give her a hug. By now she had started to really look forward to going on such an unusual and unexpected trip.

The next day at school she told Mr Sneed her good news, and he said that Ella and Jessie's parents had given them permission to go too. He added that the little girl from Siberia was called Katia, and she would be arriving in a week's time, one day before Maya and her friends left on their journey. "Miss Acres has kindly offered to escort you to Taymira Academy. She will stay there with you for a few days to get you settled and then come back to collect you when the two weeks are over."

Returning to her classroom just before lessons began, Maya took her usual place between her two best friends. Jessie was leaning forward over her desk, her wavy brown hair escaping from a pony tail and forming a curtain around her face as she doodled a frozen winter landscape on the front cover of her history book. Jessie had quite a talent for art, although her greatest gifts were in gymnastics. Despite being small for her age, like Maya, she had already won three medals in the county gymnastics trials. Quick to laughter and just as quick to quarrel over the silliest things (like whether tennis balls are green or yellow), Jessie's moods could revolve as quickly as her amazing backflips.

On Maya's other side sat Ella, who looked up from her tablet with a smile as Maya took her seat. A little more thoughtful and cautious than Maya or Jessie, Ella was a genius with technology and was never happier than when she had a laptop in front of her and a problem to solve. Her friends had often benefitted from her inventions, like the "Auto-Homework Generator" software that had made life very easy for them the previous term. With her golden hair and studious manner, she was always the last of the three to be suspected of any mischief by their teachers.

"Hi Maya," Ella greeted her friend, "so excited about Siberia! I've been reading about it – did you know it can get so cold that water poured from a boiling kettle turns to ice before it hits the ground?"

The three girls couldn't concentrate much on their lessons for the next few days. They chattered constantly about the exciting times they would have in Siberia.

"I wonder if we'll see any polar bears?" asked Maya. All three girls had a love of animals and were longing to see some of the local wildlife when they got to the Taymira Academy.

"It's possible," Ella replied, "we'll be far enough north. Huskies come from Siberia, don't they? Imagine if the school has a pet huskie…"

"Yeah, or a woolly mammoth!" Jessie added. "I remember hearing they live under the ice in Siberia."

"Erm, I don't think they actually live under the ice, Jessie," Maya explained. "It's just that they've been found preserved in ice caves."

"Preserved, exactly! So if we find one, we would just need to revive it. Can you research that please Maya, just in case? Basically 'how to thaw out a mammoth', that should do it."

"Sure, I'll make a note," Maya responded, with a wink at Ella: they were both well accustomed to Jessie's eccentric ideas.

From what she had heard about Siberia Maya only knew that it was thousands of miles away in eastern Russia, and that it would be wild and beautiful but also very cold and remote. "We can ask Katia about it when she arrives," she suggested.

At last the week went by and Katia did arrive. Maya saw her standing in the playground in the morning with a very tall, thin lady. Katia was small and pale, with dark eyes and long dark hair in a neat plait. Maya went over to speak to her.

"Hello!" she said in her friendliest voice. "You must be Katia. I'm Maya, and I will be visiting your school. I'm leaving tomorrow with my friends, and I'm very excited about it."

Katia looked as though she was about to reply, when the tall lady answered instead with a strong accent Maya didn't recognise, "Hello Maya. My name is Ms Kotka. I am looking after Katia while she is here in England. Katia is very pleased to meet you. Come Katia!" With that, she led the little girl away to the other side of the playground.

"How strange!" thought Maya, "I only wanted to welcome her. Maybe she's very shy."

At lunchtime she saw Katia again, sitting with Ms Kotka in the school hall. Maya gave her a little wave and she waved back, glancing first at her stern-faced companion. "I really wanted to talk to Katia about the Taymira Academy," she said to Jessie and Ella, "but I feel a bit scared of that Ms Kotka."

"Don't worry," said Jessie. "We'll see it for ourselves tomorrow!"

"Yes," added Ella, "and I'm actually glad Ms Kotka will be here and not over there with us. She does look a bit ferocious."

Maya and her friends spent the evening packing for their trip. They needed to take their warmest, thickest clothes, which were so bulky they each needed a grown-up sized suit-case. Maya carefully added her most precious possession, a necklace that her parents had given to her the last time she saw them. Suspended from the necklace was a delicate silver de-sign that looked like a section of a snowflake. "That will fit right in where I'm going," Maya thought to herself with a smile.

In the morning she went down to the end of the garden and found Woody, who was crouched amongst a pile of sticks near where she had left him. "Woody, I'm going out into the big wide world just like you," she told him fondly, and gave him a goodbye kiss on his little brown face. Woody seemed a bit surprised, as if he hadn't previously received a lot of kisses, but gave Maya a look that she took to mean, "Have a great time in Siberia."

Aunt Jane dropped her off at Ella's house and said her goodbyes, repeating a hundred times that she wanted Maya to call or email her every day. Jessie soon arrived too, and the three girls stood together outside Ella's house and waited for Miss Acres to arrive to take them to the airport. A large black car stopped nearby.

"Who's this pulling up?" Jessie wondered aloud. "It can't be Miss Acres, she drives a yellow car."

Then the girls had a nasty surprise. The door of the car opened and Ms Kotka got out. She smiled at them, showing two rows of sharp teeth. "Girls, I'm sorry to tell you that Miss Acres is ill. I will be taking you to Siberia instead."

YOU'VE GOT TO PICK A PASSPORT OR TWO

Maya, Ella and Jessie looked at each other in horror. They liked Miss Acres and had looked forward to making the long journey to Siberia with her to look after them. Travelling with strict Ms Kotka wouldn't be anywhere near as much fun. For a moment they hoped she might be mistaken, but Ella's mum came out and told them that the school had just called to tell her about the change of plan.

"Come, girls! We don't want to miss our flight," said Ms Kotka, opening the back door of her car and ushering them inside. Maya, Ella and Jessie got in and waved goodbye to Ella's mum, and then sat in silence as they were driven to the airport. They were still excited about going on a plane together but Ms Kotka scowled angrily at them each time they started a whispered conversation.

"I hope the other teachers in Siberia are a bit friendlier," Maya thought, a little nervously.

When they got to the airport and checked in, the girls were delighted to find that they had seats together and their companion would be several rows in front of them. "That's a relief!" Jessie said, "Now we can enjoy the flight".

Maya hadn't flown before so her friends let her have the window seat. She watched eagerly as the plane raced down the runway and soared into the air, the houses and cars below looking first like little toys, and then no more than dots as the plane climbed higher and higher. After a while they flew through some thick clouds and carried on rising until it appeared as though they had a fluffy white carpet beneath them. Maya's thoughts turned to her parents.

"It's beautiful," she murmured to herself, "but this must have been what it was like for Mum and Dad in the Arctic, nothing but white in every direction."

Their journey was so long that they had to stop and change planes at St Petersburg. "Girls!" barked Ms Kotka, "Our next plane departs in one hour. You will remain at my side and wait quietly until then."

"I wish we could find a way to shake her off," Ella grumbled. "Then we could relax."

"Maybe we can…" replied Maya thoughtfully.

Ms Kotka marched the girls to a café in the airport departure lounge and ordered a glass of water for each of them to drink. They sat in silence for a few moments until Maya suggested, "Let's all just check we still have our passports – we have to be so careful not to lose them."

Each of the girls made sure their passports were safely in their coat pockets. "Do you have yours, Ms Kotka?" Maya enquired.

"Of course I do, foolish child!" Ms Kotka snapped irritably, putting her hand up to pat her inside pocket. Then she looked confused and started checking all her other pockets and her handbag. It was clear that her passport was nowhere to be found.

The teacher tried to force a calm expression onto her face and said "Girls, I must have dropped my passport on the way here from the plane. I am going to find it – do not move a muscle until I return!" With that she jumped up and scurried away in the direction they had come from, anxiously checking the floor as she went.

"How lucky for us!" giggled Jessie with a big smile. "I hope she doesn't find it and has to stay here forever."

"Very lucky," returned Maya, "but sometimes you make your own luck." She leant forward and showed her two friends something peeping out of her sleeve. They recognised it straight away – the black cover of Ms Kotka's passport!

"I grabbed it when she reached over to get her handbag", Maya explained. "Don't worry, I'll give it back to her just before we have to catch our flight – but until then we can relax."

The girls swapped their water for strawberry milkshakes and spent a very enjoyable twenty minutes sipping and chatting, relieved from the oppressive influence of their grim companion. They were just checking the nearby screens to see if it was nearly time to leave when a boy approached them. He was a little taller than they were, but they could only guess at his age because most of his face was covered by an enormous pair of sunglasses and a thick fur-lined hat pulled as far down as it could go.

"Miss Madison?" the boy asked, looking at Jessie. "Please – I must speak with you."

"I'm Maya Madison," Maya replied. "How do you know my name?"

"I am sorry – I only knew that you were small, with the dark hair. I have seen a photo, but it was taken many years ago."

"You've seen a photo of me? But who are you? What do you want?" Maya asked, quite startled by the boy's strange appearance and by what he said.

"I met your mother and father," the boy answered hurriedly, taking off his sunglasses and glancing around. "I do not have much time. I have to warn you: please be careful in Siberia. Trust nobody. You must find a way in."

Maya had a hundred questions whirling in her mind, but before she could ask them the door of the café burst open and two men in dark suits entered. They saw the boy standing next to Maya and strode towards him. Quick as a flash the mysterious boy darted away between the tables and dived through the door leading to the café's kitchen. The two men followed him, and the girls heard a series of crashing and clanging noises coming through the door as it swung shut.

A few moments later the men reappeared. They both looked cross and one of them seemed to be wearing a trifle. They walked back out of the café exchanging angry words in

Russian, the messier of the two pausing only to lick some jelly off his sleeve. Then they were gone.

The girls looked at each other in amazement. Something told them this was going to be nothing like their previous school trip to the Thornbury Nasal Hair Trimmer Museum and Gift Shop.

ANOTHER WARNING

Ms Kotka came hurrying back to the café and asked what had caused the disturbance.

"I'm not sure, we didn't really see," replied Maya. She didn't want to tell the teacher what the boy had said to her. "Look at this though – your passport! It was under the table all along."

Maya handed Ms Kotka back her passport and the teacher grabbed it eagerly. She was so pleased to have it back she didn't ask any further questions. Instead she glanced at the departures board and announced, "Our flight is ready for boarding – girls, you will follow me."

Maya and her friends got onto the plane that was to take them on to Siberia, and were pleased to find that once again they had seats a few rows behind Ms Kotka. After take-off Maya decided to read some of the book she had brought in her hand luggage. She had been too excited to start it during the first part of their journey. She opened her shiny purple bag and was about to grab her book when she noticed a little blue envelope tucked into the bag's inside pocket.

"I don't remember putting that in there," Maya thought to herself. Taking it out, she saw that the envelope was blank. Inside, she found a short note on a small blue card:

Maya, please don't go to the Taymira Academy. It is not safe for you there. Say you have changed your mind and want to go home. Please be careful!

- K

Maya showed the card to Ella and Jessie. "Who could have put this in my bag?" she asked them. "Do you think it was that boy from the airport?"

"He was only there for a moment though," said Ella, "I don't see how he could have put that envelope in your bag without you noticing. It must have been there since we left home."

"Wait… wait… I recognise that slanted handwriting!" Jessie exclaimed, putting a finger to each of her temples and twisting them as if trying to tune in to a memory that was just out of reach. "Got it! I saw some work Katia was doing the day she came to Crinkleton. This writing looks just like hers – and the initial matches too."

"If Katia wanted to tell me something why didn't she just speak to me when we met?" Maya wondered.

"Maybe she was too frightened of horrible old Ms Kotka," suggested Ella.

"You're both probably right," Maya agreed, "so that makes two people warning us about Siberia. I wonder why?"

Her friends had no answer to this, so Maya sat back in her seat lost in thought. When she finally looked up half an hour later, she noticed Ms Kotka's head had lolled to the side and was resting on the shoulder of a big bearded man sitting on her left in the window seat. The man looked a little uncomfortable and annoyed, but Maya considered he must be too polite to wake the teacher up.

Seeing that the aisle seat on Ms Kotka's right was unoccupied, Maya nudged Jessie. "I think our Siberian friend needs a bit of fun in her life," she whispered to her friends, with a mischievous expression on her face they had seen many times before. "I've got an idea, but I need your artistic skills Jessie – come with me."

"What are you up to, Maya?" asked Ella in surprise as they quietly squeezed past her and into the aisle of the plane. "Just be careful, OK?" Cautious by nature though she was, Ella accompanied this warning with a smile. As the eldest and tallest of the three she often found herself cast as the voice of reason, and had even talked Maya out of some of her craziest schemes, but in truth she enjoyed her friend's tricks and pranks as much as anyone.

Maya and Jessie quietly made their way up the aisle to the row where Ms Kotka sat. Most of the passengers were also asleep, or engrossed in books or films, so they attracted little attention. Maya motioned for Jessie to sit down next to the teacher's slumbering form, and looked around quickly. The bearded man turned and raised a quizzical eyebrow in her direction, but she put her finger to her lips, imploring him to be like a good, soft, beardy pillow and not wake the bony sleeper. After a moment's thought, the man gave an almost imperceptible shrug and turned back to the window.

Satisfied that they would not now be disturbed, Maya reached down to the floor beneath Ms Kotka's seat and retrieved the teacher's handbag. Reaching inside she quickly

found the two things she was looking for: lipstick and mas-
cara.

"Remember that cool face painting you did for Ella last
summer?" she whispered to Jessie. "I bet our teacher would
enjoy something like that!"

Jessie's eyes widened as she understood what Maya was
suggesting, but after a moment's hesitation her boundless
bravery quelled any doubts and she took the makeup from
Maya with an impish sparkle in her eye. Then she got to work,
and was soon frowning with concentration as she gave Ms
Kotka a unique makeover, using the most delicate of touches
to avoid waking her.

Maya squeezed into the seat alongside Jessie and kept
watch for the stewardesses, or anyone else who might spoil
their fun. Her heart raced as she considered how the teacher
would react if she woke up at that moment, but she found herself enjoying that feeling of the danger of discovery almost as
much as the prank itself. After what seemed an eternity Jessie
turned away from her masterpiece and gently clicked the lids
back onto the makeup tubes before slipping them back into the
handbag.

"Wow Jessie, that's your best one yet!" whispered Maya in admiration, leaning over to get a better look. The severe features of their companion were now greatly improved by the addition of whiskers, a little black nose and an ear-to-ear grin that was comically at odds with the pinch-mouthed glare they were accustomed to seeing.

"OK, that's enough time admiring my work, let's move!" replied Jessie, poking Maya in the ribs. Maya gave Ms Kotka's bearded neighbour a conspiratorial wink (mentally upgrading him from "weirdy beardy-face guy" to "cool beardy-face guy") and they sneaked back to their seats.

Ella was waiting impatiently to hear exactly what they had done. "Let me guess – the full Cheshire cat?"

"Just wait till you see it!" Maya replied. "Ms Kotka doesn't carry it off quite like you did at your party last summer, but still – it's quite a sight…"

At that moments the seatbelt signs came on, and a few minutes later the plane touched down in the evening darkness at the airport in Siberia.

TO TAYMIRA

Maya and her friends followed Ms Kotka through security and baggage collection. The teacher attracted a few quizzical looks from the airport staff, but she was too absorbed in hurrying the girls along to notice.

Once they had their luggage they went out through the glass doors at the main entrance to the airport. Although it was only late afternoon it was very dark, and fluffy snowflakes were slowly drifting down from the sky. The girls were glad they had their warmest coats on as they patiently waited next to their frosty companion, who wore a much thinner grey jacket but didn't seem to feel the cold.

After a few minutes a black jeep with tinted windows pulled up next to them. Ms Kotka ushered the children into the back seat and then got into the passenger seat at the front. "Attention girls!" she turned to them and said, "This is Dr Stoker, the Director of Taymira Academy".

The driver of the car turned to them and smiled. He was a big, red-faced man with short grey hair and little round glasses with silver frames.

"Maya, Jessie and Ella," he said in a booming voice, looking at each of them in turn, "welcome to Siberia! Ms Kotka has told me all about you: what clever little girls you are and how lucky we are to have you visiting our humble school."

Maya was surprised by several things: the doctor knowing their names, his friendly greeting, his English accent, and most of all the idea that Ms Kotka might have said anything nice about her or her friends.

He turned to his colleague and remarked jovially, "It looks like you've had lots of fun on the journey over!" indicating towards the manically grinning feline features Jessie had given her.

Ms Kotka reached up and adjusted the passenger mirror so she could see what Dr Stoker meant. A look of intense anger passed across her face as she saw what they had done, and Maya felt herself tensing up in readiness for the recriminations that would follow. To her surprise, however, the teacher seemed to quell her rage and even forced an unnatural smile onto her face. "The girls like a little joke," she responded through gritted teeth.

"Can't believe she let us off," Jessie whispered to Maya, as Dr Stoker pulled out into the snowy street. "Maybe she's not as bad as we thought."

"Perhaps… or maybe she just didn't want to admit to her boss she was sleeping on the job," Maya replied quietly. "I guess we'll find out soon enough."

They drove through light traffic to the edge of the town, then continued out into the dark countryside. Through the window Maya saw white hills glistening in the moonlight, and could just make out the gloomy shadows of a few trees as they sped past. Soon there were no other cars in sight ahead or behind, and all was quiet except the low hum of the engine of Dr Stoker's jeep, and a slushing sound from the tires as they span through the snow gathering on the road.

"Is it far to the Academy?" she asked sleepily, suddenly very tired after her long journey.

"Not far, not far at all," said the Doctor, soothingly, "but why don't you get some rest?"

Maya saw that Ella and Jessie were asleep already, so she put her head on Ella's shoulder and let herself drift away into a deep sleep.

THE ACADEMY

Maya was awoken by the feeling of the car coming to a stop. She was quite glad to be awake, after restless dreams in which Ms Kotka chased her around and around a giant strawberry milkshake. Glancing at her watch she found that they had been driving for many hours.

Looking out of the window she saw they had arrived in front of two large buildings in the middle of the bleak and frozen countryside. The buildings were both five stories high, but one looked quite old with crumbling brickwork while the other looked brand new and had gleaming metallic walls which reflected the headlights of their car.

"Behold your new home, girls" said Ms Kotka, looking genuinely happy for the first time since they had met her.

"Welcome to the Taymira Academy!" added Dr Stoker. "Ms Kotka will look after you from here."

"You will follow me," commanded Ms Kotka, opening her door. "Bring your luggage with you, please."

The girls got out of the car and took their suitcases from the boot, then followed Ms Kotka through heavy oak doors into the older building. Inside was a reception desk, behind which sat four young men in smart grey uniforms. The first two looked very professional, and were busy checking a row of monitors and making notes. The third was larger with a heavy monobrow, and was patiently sharpening a pile of pencils using a sharpener that looked ridiculously small in his meaty hands. The last man, little more than a boy in age and stature, was picking his nose when they entered but when he saw Ms Kotka he hastily wiped his hand on his big colleague's jacket and stood to attention. Ms Kotka exchanged a few words with them and then led the girls towards a staircase.

Ella nudged Maya and pointed to a security camera in the corner of the reception area, which turned to follow them as they walked across the floor. "It looks like it must be very safe here, with all these cameras and people watching the doors," she said.

"Somehow it doesn't make me feel very safe," thought Maya, but she said nothing and helped Ella heave her suitcase up the steep stairs. Ms Kotka led them all the way to the top floor and then along a dark corridor and into a large dormitory.

Maya had never seen such a long room, with two rows of identical bunk beds stretching away down each side as far as she could see in the dim light.

It was well after bed time, and in most of the beds nearby she could see that little girls her own age were fast asleep. As Ms Kotka hurried them down to the far end of the room she saw one or two pairs of eyes peeping out at her as she passed. Finally they arrived at two empty bunk beds, which stood at the end of one row. "Girls, these are your beds. See your names on the display. I expect you to be in bed asleep in five minutes," Ms Kotka instructed them, then turned and marched back out of the room.

Sure enough, each bed had a little display screen on the wall next to it, showing a name, the time, and some more information in Russian that Maya could not read. She saw her name next to the top bunk of the last bed, with Jessie's by the bunk below her and Ella's by the top bunk of the next bed. Maya wondered if the other girls in the dorm would start talking now their teacher had left, but the room remained completely still and quiet except for a few gentle snores.

The girls got changed into their pyjamas quickly and stored their suitcases under their beds. After they had climbed under their covers and lain there for a couple of minutes Jessie whispered, "I'm cold and lonely."

"Me too," Maya and Ella agreed.

"Why don't you come up here just for the first night?" Maya suggested, so her two friends climbed up the little ladder to her bunk and fell asleep lying head to toe like a tin of sardines.

THE FIRST DAY

Maya was awakened by a loud buzzing noise coming from a speaker next to her bed-side display. Glancing at the screen Maya saw that the time was 6AM, much earlier than she was used to getting up at home. Looking around she noticed that all the other girls in the dormitory had already started to get dressed.

"Come on sleepy heads," she nudged Jessie and Ella, "We had better get going, we don't want to be late on our first day."

They got dressed and then watched the others. Each of the Taymira girls quickly and quietly got dressed in identical grey uniforms and made their bed perfectly, then scraped back their hair into a tight bun and stood to attention at the end of their beds.

Maya waved and smiled at some of the girls but got little response. Only a slender girl from the bunk opposite hers gave her a shy smile as she went about her preparation for the day. The girl had long fair hair which she had to work hard to get into a neat bun like the others. Maya saw from her bedside screen that her name was Adelina.

"Maybe we should tie up our hair?" Jessie suggested.

"Yes, let's," Maya agreed. She and Jessie helped each other to do as they had seen their new classmates do and soon had quite neat and tidy buns. However, when they tried to do the same with Ella's long, wavy blonde hair they struggled.

"My hair never wants to go into a bun," Ella explained. "I'll just have to put it in a ponytail instead, it won't matter."

When they were ready Maya, Ella and Jessie stood at the end of their beds and waited like the other girls. A few minutes later Ms Kotka appeared and stalked down between the two lines of children, examining the students and their beds. She seemed content with what she saw until she got to the end of the room, where Maya and her friends were standing nervously.

"Adelina, your bed is a disgrace!" she haughtily informed the girl opposite Maya, and made a note in a little black book she produced from her pocket. Adelina hurried to straighten her pillow as Ms Kotka turned to Maya. She stared at her for what seemed like an eternity before moving on to Ella.

"Here at Taymira we keep our hair tidy," she said severely, giving Ella's blonde curls a sharp yank and pointing to her own grey hair which was scraped back so tightly it looked painful. Getting out her notebook she made another entry, and then strode to the door and clapped her hands. Maya and Ella exchanged a silent look of surprise and alarm – none of their teachers back home would dream of pulling a child's hair. The girls began filing out of the room in a quiet and orderly manner, with Maya at the back next to Adelina.

"Hello," she said with a smile, "I'm Maya. Do you speak English? I'm afraid I don't speak any Russian."

"Yes, I understand a little English," the girl replied. Maya saw that she looked sad and asked why.

"My name is in Ms Kotka's book," Adelina explained.

"Is that bad?" asked Maya, "I think my friend Ella's name is in there too."

"Yes… it is bad," Adelina answered gravely, "You have seen the new building next door? It is called The Taymira Scientific Research Institute. There are labs there, and when we are in trouble we are sent to help with the experiments."

"That doesn't sound *too* bad," said Maya, hopefully.

"Yes, but 'helping' with the experiments usually means they do their latest tests on us. It is a very scary place to go."

"Are all Russian teachers as strict as Ms Kotka?" Maya asked. "She's a bit different from what we're used to."

"Actually she is from Finland, like me," Adelina replied. "But of all the teachers in this school I think she is one of the worst: it seems like she enjoys punishing us."

"I must find a way to get Ella's name out of that book," thought Maya, "and Adelina's too if I can. I don't want anybody experimenting on them!"

THE CUPBOARD CAPER

The girls went downstairs to a large and gloomy dining hall on the first floor and had a simple breakfast of porridge, then followed the other children into their first lesson. Maya and her friends sat at three empty desks near the front of the classroom. A few minutes later Ms Kotka appeared and Maya's heart sank: she had been hoping they might have a different teacher this morning.

Ms Kotka said a few words to the class in Russian then, to Maya's surprise, placed a bucket and a banjo on the large teacher's desk in front of the blackboard.

Looking around she saw the other children getting paper and pencils out of their desks, and realised that the subject must be art. Ms Kotka turned to her and said "Girls, you will sketch these objects. Maya, you will find paper for you and your friends in the supply room at the back."

She pointed to a door in the far corner of the room. As she did so, Maya noticed that the teacher took her notepad out of her pocket and placed it on the desk in front of her. "Maybe this is my chance," Maya thought to herself, "but how to get hold of it?" As she turned to go and get the paper she whispered, "Notepad!" to Jessie, and then walked slowly to the back of the room, thinking as fast as she could.

She went through the supply room door and closed it behind her. It was small, little larger than a cupboard, with shelves reaching up to the ceiling holding various stationery and art equipment. Right in front of Maya were the pencils, and next to them a neat stack of art paper.

Glancing around, Maya saw a step ladder leaning against the wall, obviously placed there to allow the girls to access items on the higher shelves. Moving as quickly and quietly as she could, Maya gathered up all the pencils and used the step ladder to put them on the very highest shelf. Then she folded the step ladder and slid it under the bottom shelf, out of sight.

Opening the supply room door, she called to the teacher, "Excuse me Ms Kotka, I can't reach the pencils."

"Nonsense, you foolish child!" Ms Kotka replied. "They are right in front of you. We always keep them close to hand."

"I'm sorry but they aren't," Maya explained, "they're right on the top shelf."

"Then use the step ladder," came the abrupt response.

"But I can't see a step ladder…" said Maya, then tried to keep a smile off her face as Ms Kotka rose from her seat and stomped angrily across the room towards her. When she stepped inside the supply room, the teacher's tall and angular figure seemed to fill the small space from top to bottom and made Maya feel quite stifled.

"The pencils have been moved, and I am *most certain* there was a step ladder in here," Ms Kotka said sharply, peering around her in the dim light. Maya waited nervously, certain that she would be in big trouble if Ms Kotka found she had hidden the ladder. Luckily, she gave up looking after a few moments and snatched the pencils from the top shelf, handed them to Maya and marched back to her desk without another word.

Maya hoped her friends had understood that she was trying to distract the teacher so they could get to the notebook. After bringing the pencils and paper back to her desk she glanced enquiringly at Jessie. Jessie winked at her and patted the pocket of her dress.

The girls set about the task of drawing the bucket and banjo. Maya was feeling quite pleased with her efforts until she glanced across and saw Jessie's masterpiece – an incredibly lifelike depiction of Ms Kotka as a grubby street performer, dejectedly strumming her banjo while happy children threw spare change into her bucket. "Well," Jessie whispered, "she didn't say we had to draw *just* those things…"

After an hour or two the dull clanging of a bell announced the end of the lesson. The girls were told it was "recreation time" for the next ten minutes, and were ushered into a cold courtyard in the middle of the school.

"Well done Maya!" said Ella as soon as they were alone. "I'm so glad my name's not in that horrid notebook any more. Jessie just got back in her seat before Ms Kotka came back, with not a moment to spare!"

Jessie pulled a crumpled piece of paper from her pocket and showed it to them. She had torn out the whole page, as neatly as she could. The girls couldn't understand most of the writing on the page, but they could see Ella and Adelina's names near the top. Adelina was standing nearby, still looking miserable, so Maya waved her over and showed her the page.

"Look," she encouraged her new friend, "I bet Ms Kotka won't remember to send you to the lab without this. She puts so many names in her book I'm sure she won't notice one page missing."

Adelina's eyes filled with tears of gratitude. "Thank you... all of you... you are so brave to do this. My brother Tao disobeyed a teacher and got sent to the lab. I have been too afraid to do anything but follow orders since then. I must try to have courage like you, Maya."

"I'm sure you're just as brave as we are," said Maya, "but this school drains it out of you. What a shame you can't come back with us when we leave in two weeks' time – you would enjoy Crinkleton School a lot more!"

SLIME

After ten cold minutes of recreation the class had a tricky Maths lesson that was followed by lunch in the draughty dining hall. The girls lined up for their food and were given the same as all the other children: rice, chicken, beans, a drink of water and of course a bowl of green slime.

Maya found a place next to Adelina at one of the long tables in the hall, and asked, "What on earth is this funny looking green gloop? Is it some sort of Russian dessert?"

Adelina dropped her voice so nobody else could overhear, and replied, "No, it is not dessert. It is our vitamin supplement. They make it in the lab. They say it is good for us."

"What does it taste like?" asked Jessie, who was sitting opposite.

"It does not taste good," Adelina admitted. "Sometimes it makes me feel sick. It changes every few weeks, but it is always bad."

Maya poked the green slime with her spoon. It wobbled around in the bowl in a most unpleasant manner. "Will we get in trouble if we don't eat it?" she asked.

"Yes," Adelina explained, "you will go back in the teacher's notebook."

"Well, I'm not eating it," announced Ella. "We have to get rid of it somehow."

Looking around, Maya saw Dr Stoker sitting at a table at the end of the room with some female teachers, on a raised platform allowing them to watch the children as they ate. "Leave this to me," she told the other girls, and emptied all four bowls of slime into the beaker she had been drinking from.

Concealing the beaker in the folds of her dress, Maya then approached Dr Stoker's table. The Academy Director was drinking a black coffee while going over some paperwork, and gave her the insincere smile she remembered from their first meeting as she approached. "Ah, young Maya," he greeted her. "Allow me to introduce Professor De Molle and Professor Farrell, two of the academy's finest teachers. Ladies, this is Maya Madison, visiting us from England."

Professor De Molle favoured Maya with a haughty nod, the unnaturally tight skin of her face quite expressionless. Professor Farrell parted her long ginger fringe and barked a muffled, "Hello!" through a mouthful of sausage.

"Can I help you with something, Maya?" Stoker continued.

"Yes," Maya replied, with a sweet smile of her own. "I was wondering if we could use the telephone to call our families, to let them know we've arrived safely and how nice it is here?"

"I'm sorry, that won't be possible," Dr Stoker replied. "The phone lines are down. We suffer with this a lot because our school is so remote. I will let you know as soon as it can be arranged."

"He's lying, I'm sure I saw a guy on reception using the phone on our way here from class," Maya thought to herself. "Well, at least he's helped me decide what to do with this slime!"

A few minutes later Maya came back to her seat and put the empty beaker on the table. "Where's all the gunk gone?" asked Jessie.

"Wait until the teachers leave and you might see," Maya replied with a mischievous grin.

Ella and Jessie tried to watch the teachers' table without making their interest too obvious. A few minutes later Dr Stoker rose to leave, deep in conversation with another member of staff. Taking his coat and briefcase from the chair next to him he strode to the door of the hall.

For a moment the girls didn't notice anything unusual, until Jessie pointed to the floor behind Dr Stoker. A thin trail of green slime was following the Academy Director from the room. Looking closer they saw that it was coming from his briefcase.

"Maya!" gasped Ella, "Tell me you didn't put it in Dr Stoker's briefcase!"

"It may have slipped in there somehow," Maya replied with a smile.

"But why?" asked Jessie. "I mean, he seems a lot nicer than Ms Kotka, at least."

"I don't trust him," Maya explained, "He wasn't honest about how far we had to come from the airport, and now he's saying we can't call our families. This is a horrid school, and he's in charge of it. He wants all the children to eat this weird slime... well, maybe he should try some himself!"

Jessie nodded in agreement, but Ella added, "I just hope you don't get in trouble, Maya. He's sure to guess it was you."

"I'm not worried," said Maya, "We'll be back home before you know it. How much trouble can I possibly get into?"

EXTREME EXPERIMENTS

After lunch Adelina told the girls it was time for a Science lesson. "This is our least favourite lesson," she added.

"Why's that?" asked Maya, "I've always enjoyed Science... I suppose it's because my parents were scientists. I remember pouring over the periodic table before I even started school, so I could be just like them when I grew up. At Crinkleton we've done some really fun projects like making volcanoes and glaciers – don't you do that sort of thing here?"

"You'll see," replied Adelina gloomily, and they filed into the science room. It was very different from the rest of the school, with an abundance of computers and hi-tech equipment arranged on neat rows of lab tables. The room and everything in it looked very new and very expensive.

"At least it's warm in here," Ella whispered to Maya as they took their seats at one of the free tables. The softly humming equipment, along with the thick new doors and tinted windows, combined to create an unpleasantly hot and airless atmosphere in stark contrast to their chilly dormitory.

A plump man with black curly hair and a long white lab coat strode into the science room and took his place at the front of the class. He spoke a few words to the class in Russian and then turned to Maya and her friends. "Welcome, English students. My name is Mr Karkiv. I am head of Science. You will be a great help to the school by joining in our studies here. Adelina will show you what to do." With those words, the teacher seated himself in front of a bank of computer screens and spoke no further.

"Isn't he going to teach you anything?" Maya whispered to Adelina. "How will you know what to do?"

"It is always the same, that is how we know," Adelina explained.

Looking around the room, Maya saw that all the girls and boys had split into pairs. One child in each pair put on a heavy helmet with red lenses at the front that fitted over their eyes. The helmets were connected by thick cables to a black box mounted on each table, which whirred noisily and displayed rows of flashing lights. The second child pressed some switches on the box, and the girls watched in surprise as the helmets vibrated and the lenses lit up with an orange glow.

"What on earth are those things for? Doesn't all that shaking hurt your head?" Ella asked Adelina.

"We do not really know what they are for," Adelina replied. "We are just told to put them on, and then we have to send the results to the laboratories in the building next door. It doesn't hurt, but it makes us feel a bit sick."

"Girls!" Mr Karkiv called over, "Please proceed with your lesson. Copy the others."

"It's not much of a lesson if we don't even know what the machine is for," grumbled Maya.

"I'm scared to put that helmet on," said Jessie, "It looks horrible, like it's going to fry my brain. Don't let them give me a crispy fried brain, Maya!"

"Don't worry, I'll go first," Maya reassured her, "I'm sure it's not that bad."

She hoisted the heavy equipment onto her head and fastened the straps underneath her chin. It was just as uncomfortable as it looked. Jessie reluctantly pressed the buttons they had seen the other girls use, and Maya braced herself. The whirring noise from the black box slowly increased, and then the lenses over Maya's eyes lit up, making her blink. A moment later though, the orange light flashed and went off, and the black box went back to a low hum, displaying several red warning lights. Looking over at the table where Ella and Adelina had paired up, Maya saw that the same thing had happened to Ella.

A soft beeping noise came from one of Mr Karkiv's displays, and he looked up in annoyance. He checked some numbers on the screen and then got to his feet and came over to look at the units next to Jessie and Adelina. After tapping a few buttons, he restarted the experiment and Maya saw her lenses start to glow once again. Just like before, however, the machines shut down after a few moments.

"Girls," Mr Karkiv asked in his flat, expressionless voice, "You were given your nutrients at lunch time, yes? And you took them, like the other children?"

Jessie and Ella looked at the floor nervously, but Maya answered for them. "You mean the green slime? Yes, we all had it. It was delicious! I do wish we were given slime for lunch every day back home."

Mr Karkiv glanced at her but appeared not to note any sarcasm in her voice. "The equipment may be faulty," he concluded. "I will file a report. You must sit quietly until the end of class."

Looking around the classroom Maya was very glad that the experiment had not worked on her or her friends. After sitting under the strange helmet for half an hour, each of their classmates swapped with their partners. Many of the children looked quite dizzy and confused when their turn was over. "I'm not surprised after all that shaking and flashing," Jessie whispered. "I feel ill just watching them."

"You know everything about technology, Ella," suggested Maya as they watched, "Is there anything you can do to shut down those machines?"

Ella thought for a second, taking a closer look at the box on her desk that the cable from the helmet plugged into. "I bet this is actually just a normal computer in an industrial casing," she explained after a moment's consideration. "I probably could do something with it but we don't have a screen – it looks like it's connected to one of those monitors above Karkiv's head. If I start messing with it he's bound to notice."

"Just tell me how long you need," Maya replied with a determined smile.

SHUT DOWN

It wouldn't be easy to buy Ella the time she needed to work her magic on the sinister scientific devices, but there was no way Maya was going to leave their new classmates to suffer any longer if she could help it.

"Two minutes should do it," Ella told her, frowning and flicking her eyes from side to side as she always did when turning over a problem in her mind. "I see a keyboard over there I can grab – but what are you going to do about Mr Karkiv?"

"I've got an idea," Maya explained, "but I need some food, or drink, or something... do we have anything?"

Her friends shook their heads. "Sorry," said Jessie unhappily, "we've got absolutely nothing. It's a long shot, but maybe there's something in these drawers."

Their workstation had two wide drawers with stainless steel handles, which the girls gently pulled open. Inside were row after row of neatly arranged glass beakers with metal lids, bearing labels in both Russian and English.

"Not exactly what I was hoping for, but let's see what we've got," Maya encouraged her friends.

Jessie ran her finger along the first row of beakers. "OK, so – hydrogen peroxide, sodium chloride, iron filings, corn flour, zinc, sodium cyanide, dihydrogen monoxide… anything we can use, Maya?"

"Not a great start," Maya replied. "They use hydrogen peroxide to make teeth whiteners but it also explodes if you're not careful with it. Sodium cyanide is a deadly poison, and sodium chloride is basically salt. The zinc wouldn't be great for me either if I had any more than the tiniest amount. That last beaker is fine though – it's just another name for water. Let's keep looking."

"What about these?" asked Jessie, pointing to some more beakers on the third row. "Extract of lemon, extract of lime – at least they won't kill you."

"Thanks, Jessie, this might just do it!" Maya hissed excitedly, trying to keep her voice down. She grabbed the lemon extract, the corn flour and an empty beaker, mixed them together and then added a little of the water. Mr Karkiv was still engrossed by the output on his monitors and ignored them, much to Maya's relief. She swirled the mixture in her beaker until it became what could only be described as yellow gloop.

"You're not really going to eat that, are you Maya?" asked Ella. "And even if you do – how will it help?"

"Don't worry about that," answered Maya, "just rest assured that in a moment you'll get the diversion you need to hack these headsets from hell."

Crouching down behind the lab table, she poured the contents of the beaker into her mouth. The strong flavour of lemon wasn't unpleasant, although the texture made her think of cold snot. Standing back up, she made a loud moaning noise and approached the teacher's desk at the front of the room. At first Mr Karkiv paid her no attention, so she deliberately stumbled into an empty stool, sending it crashing to the ground.

Mr Karkiv looked up in surprise. From the resigned, miserable obedience she had seen so far amongst the other children Maya guessed it was unusual for anyone to leave their seat until ordered to do so.

"Miss Madison - what are you doing? Please return to your desk!" the teacher exclaimed. Expecting her to comply instantly, he turned back to his displays as soon as he had spoken. Noticing some activity on the monitor immediately above his head, Maya realised that Ella had begun to work her magic on the computer and waved her arms frantically to divert Mr Karkiv's attention.

"Mmmmmmhhh!" she gurgled, pointing at her mouth.

Mr Karkiv turned back to her, now visibly annoyed. "Have you gone mad, child?" he inquired. "I will call your class supervisor – Ms Kotka."

That was the last thing Maya wanted. Gesturing to her mouth and rubbing her tummy, she conveyed the idea to their teacher that she was feeling unwell. Suddenly lurching forward, she painted a most convincing picture of a person about to be sick.

This certainly brought a reaction from Mr Karkiv, to whom the equipment on his desk was obviously precious. He attempted to shield his notes, laptop and tablet from his nauseous pupil and shouted, "Somebody please escort this girl to the medical facility!"

Turning back to the class for a moment, Maya saw Ella stowing the keyboard back on the spare desk where they had found it. Taking this as an indication her friend was finished, she span around to face the teacher and delivered the coup-de-grace.

"Mmmmh! Mmmmhh-bluuuurgh!"

With a final lunge and spasm Maya sprayed the teacher's desk, notepad and jacket with the mouthful of yellow goop she had concocted. Collapsing on the floor she took a few moments to make sure Ella was back in her seat and then announced she was feeling much better.

Mr Karkiv was standing with his head in his hands, and seemed to take a minute to come to terms with what had just happened. Eventually he snapped out of it and began racing around to find paper towels and cleaning products with which he could try to soak up the pus-like substance that was now clinging to most of his desk and clothing.

"Maya," he called sharply over his shoulder, "please return to your seat and *do not move* for the rest of the lesson. Class – continue with your experiments, immediately! We must have no more disturbances."

The other children had stopped to watch the unexpected interruption in stunned surprise. As she returned to her desk Maya thought she saw one or two children give her a look of sympathy, while a few others seemed more amused at seeing their teacher coated in slime judging by the suppressed smiles curling the very corners of their mouths. They said very little however, and soon their helmets were whirring away on their heads just as they had been before.

"What happened?" Maya whispered to Ella when Mr Karkiv had settled down and was watching his monitors again. "I was hoping you might find a way to switch off all of these machines."

"That would be too obvious," explained Ella. "I've set up a script that will wipe every computer in this room, but I've scheduled it to run in an hour, after our lesson is over. Hopefully they won't guess it was us if we have a good alibi!"

After all the other children had finished the experiment the class sat in silence while Mr Karkiv looked at the results. Maya put her hand up and asked, "Excuse me, sir, what can we learn from this lesson?"

Mr Karkiv looked at her in surprise, and replied, "Today the other children have been a great help in the search for scientific knowledge. That is all you need to know at this moment. It is a shame you and your friends could not participate."

SOME BAD NEWS

At long last the science lesson was over and Adelina told Maya and her friends that it was the last subject of the day. Their new classmate was very happy to hear Ella's prediction that it would take at least a couple of days to get the science lab back in working order after her script fired up and crippled the computers. "Just don't tell anyone it was us, OK?" Maya requested. "Not even the other girls, just to be on the safe side. I bet the teachers here have all kinds of ways to get information when they want it, so it's best if nobody knows."

They had an hour of free time before their evening meal and planned to spend it exploring the school, until Ms Kotka approached them in the corridor and said, "Girls, please follow me."

She lead them to the entrance hall of the school and then down a long corridor and through a grand oaken double door. Dr Stoker sat before them behind a broad, old fashioned desk with a red leather surface. His shiny silver laptop looked out of place in what Maya realised must be the principal's office, surrounded by antique furniture and dusty bookshelves.

"Ah, my friends from England," Dr Stoker said with a sly smile on seeing them. "Thank you for coming to see me. I have some good news for you. Your stay here with us at the Taymira Academy is to be extended. You will now be with us for six weeks, instead of just two."

Maya and her friends exchanged looks of horror. Six weeks away from home, and six weeks at this dismal school! Maya saw Jessie blink back tears at the thought, and felt like crying herself but tried to keep her voice even as she replied, "Our families won't leave us to stay here for that long."

"Nonsense Maya!" replied Dr Stoker, "I have spoken to all your parents and they are very happy for you to remain here for six weeks, or even longer."

Maya frowned. "I thought you said the phones weren't working," she reminded the Doctor.

"Yes… yes. There were some problems with the phones but now they are working again. I would let you call your families right now, but of course it is still much too early back in England. Maybe we will arrange that for tomorrow, or the next day."

"I don't want to stay here for six weeks," sobbed Jessie, "Please let us go home right now!"

"Come now," replied Dr Stoker, "We don't like to see our students unhappy. Ms Kotka, please make sure Jessie gets some extra maths work tomorrow to take her mind off it."

Maya was very unhappy at the thought of spending even longer at the strange school, but she could see there was no point in arguing further. Dr Stoker dismissed them and they trudged miserably back to their dormitory, Maya and Ella each with an arm around Jessie. "There must be some mistake," Ella insisted, "There's no way my parents would let me stay here for six weeks, especially without asking if I liked it!"

"I don't believe he talked to our families at all," Maya replied thoughtfully, "He said he had spoken with all our parents, but he obviously can't have spoken to mine."

"But why would he want us to stay here so long?" asked Jessie.

"I don't know, but I'm going to find out," Maya answered, "There's something sinister about this school, and the less time we spend here, the better."

TAYMIRA BY NIGHT

As the girls unenthusiastically nibbled at their plain and tasteless evening meal, Maya suggested their next move. "Let's wait until everyone is asleep in bed, then slip out and have a proper look around this school. Maybe we can find a way to contact home and ask our families to get us out of here as soon as possible."

Just as Maya had expected, Jessie loved the idea of sneaking around at night and agreed to the plan at once. She had thought that Ella might need more persuading, but to Maya's surprise there was no resistance from her more cautious friend.

"I will feel a lot better if we can even just send an email to our families," Ella explained, "and I just don't believe Dr Stoker is ever going to let us get in touch with them. We have to be really careful though – who knows what will happen if we get caught, after the trouble we've caused already!"

Although they had noticed the previous night that most of the children went to sleep quite early, the three friends agreed they would wait until midnight to begin their expedition. They had no way of knowing whether any teachers or other academy staff would still be up at that time, but as Maya remarked, midnight seemed the perfect time to set out on any daring mission.

Once they were in bed and all was quiet in the long, dark dormitory, the excitement of not knowing what they would find and the hope of discovering a way to contact her aunt and uncle made it easy for Maya to stay awake until the agreed time. As soon as the time on the faintly glowing display next to her bed flicked over from "23:59" to "00:00", she quietly lowered herself down the steps from her top bunk and first nudged Jessie (who had somehow fallen fast asleep) and then Ella in the next bed over.

As previously agreed, they quickly exchanged their pyjamas for their darkest clothes. For Maya and Ella this was a plain grey t-shirt with black leggings, while for Jessie it was a navy t-shirt with stripy blue jeans. "Jessie, you utter spoon head!" hissed Ella in mild annoyance. "You didn't say your darkest t-shirt had a massive sparkly sequined heart in the middle of it... you may as well be waving a glow stick!"

"Oh yeah…" replied Jessie, looking down and running her hand through her wavy brown hair in consternation. "What can I say? – I like bright colours."

"Just turn it inside out," suggested Maya.

Once Jessie had done this her friends agreed she looked suitably ready to be stealthy, and the three of them began to tip-toe towards the door at the far end of the long room.

Maya saw Adelina turn to watch sleepily as they went past her bed, and put her finger to her lips with a conspiratorial wink. The other girls seemed fast asleep, and they made it to the dormitory door without attracting any attention. Once out in the empty corridor they relaxed a little, and Maya motioned for her friends to follow her to a nearby staircase. They had deliberately chosen a narrow flight of stairs at the back of the school building rather than the main stairs at the front, having noticed that the teachers rarely used them. Easing open the creaky door to the stairwell as quietly as she could, Maya was about to descend when a hand suddenly gripped her shoulder.

Maya's heart skipped a beat, and she span around in fright. To her relief, she found it was only Ella who had grabbed her and was now pointing at the stairs in front of them.

"Don't startle me like that, Ella!" she remonstrated. "I nearly lost my lunch with shock! What's the problem?"

Ella put her finger to her lips and pointed again. On the wall a little way below the top landing where they stood there was a dot of red light, and squinting her eyes in the gloom to make out where it came from Maya recognised the unpleasant shape of a security camera.

"Thanks Ella," she whispered hoarsely, "that would have been pointing right at us as soon as we got to the bottom of this flight of stairs! It must be one of the cameras that feeds all those screens the guards on the front desk look at."

"What do we do?" asked Ella, uncertainly. "Go back? But I bet the front stairs have them too, we just haven't noticed."

"We could just hurry past it and hope for the best," suggested Jessie, as optimistic as ever. "Remember how many screens those guards had – they can't watch all of them at once."

"I know what you mean," Ella replied, "but there won't be much activity at this time with everyone in bed. Any movement could easily catch their eye."

Maya had been lost in thought for a moment, but now hesitantly offered her idea. "OK, wait… I think I have a plan, but it could be a bit dangerous."

She walked over to the banisters on the side of the landing immediately above the camera, slipping her elasticated hairband out of her hair as she did so. She then reached down and pulled off one of her socks before turning back to her friends, her long brown hair cascading forward now it was released from its pony tail. "Are you thinking what I'm thinking?"

"Let's see," replied Jessie after a pause, "wild hair, one sock on your foot and one on your hand… is the plan that you pretend you're a crazed imbecile, and while they worry about restraining you, Ella and I get to explore the school?"

"That's actually not a bad plan," Maya acknowledged with a smile, "but no. I need you to lower me over this banister."

"Maybe you *are* a crazed imbecile!" exclaimed Ella. "You do realise it's nearly a twenty foot drop down to the next floor don't you? If we dropped you…"

"Don't worry," Maya reassured her, "I appreciate your concern for my safety, but I'm really confident you won't drop me. We all want to find out more about this hellhole don't we? So just grab a leg each and let's go!"

Predictably, Jessie soon added her support for the idea, and a few minutes later Maya found herself suspended upside down from the edge of the landing, with her friends each clinging on to one of her ankles above. From this angle the stairs below did look a long way away, but Maya forced herself to focus on her task. Stretching out her right hand she could just reach the camera and tried to slip her sock over it, but it was a very awkward manoeuvre.

"Swing me forward a bit," she whispered to Jessie and Ella.

Ella muttered further complaints about the sanity of what they were doing, but with a huge effort they managed to swing Maya forward just enough to get a proper grip on the camera and slide the sock over it. On the next swing she put the hair band over the top of the sock, holding it in place.

"Now get back up here before you kill all of us!" hissed Jessie, heaving Maya's leg up as hard as she could. Jessie was surprisingly strong for her size, and moments later Maya was back on the landing with them. All three of them were out of breath from the exertion, and sat on the top step for a second to recover.

Eventually, Maya broke the silence. "After all that, nothing's going to stop us finding out what's going on around here. Let's keep going!"

They rose, and crept quietly down the stairs and into the darkness below.

TOILET HUMOUR

Keeping a careful lookout for any more cameras, the girls made their way down to the third floor. They hadn't seen more than a glimpse of it up until now, and were eager to explore.

Opening the door from the stairwell, they found themselves looking down a long corridor that ran the whole length of the school building, with dull grey doors at regular intervals. Unlike the floor above where the children slept, the corridor was well lit with strip lights placed at regular intervals.

They felt a bit exposed by the bright light and the lack of hiding places if anyone should appear, but decided to press on and see what they could find.

"If anybody comes, we can just play the dumb English tourists," Maya suggested. "We can say 'Sorry mate, came down the wrong apples and pears', that should confuse them."

"It would certainly confuse me," Ella agreed, as they slowly advanced down the corridor. "Now keep your voices down and have a look at this."

They were standing in front of the first door opening off the corridor. A small name plate was mounted on it a little way above their heads, which read "Mr Valentine Karkiv". Turning, they saw that the door opposite bore a plate of its own, marked "Professor Coco De Molle".

"This floor must be where the teachers live," Ella concluded. "We can't stay here long, or we're sure to be caught."

"Let's just carry on a little further," Maya urged her friends. She didn't want to miss any chance to find out more about the strange place that fate had stranded them in.

They tip-toed even more carefully now, rarely speaking except to read the names on the doors they passed.

"Dr Fenny Le Freen"

"Mr Charles Thornton-Blinkhorne"

"Professor Hattie Farrell"

"Mr Sükhbaataryn Uugan"

"The teachers here must come from all over the world, judging by their names," whispered Maya, "and look, here's our all-time fave."

The sign on the next door read "Ms Inhottava Kotka".

"Inhottava? She has the look of an 'Inhottava' somehow," commented Jessie. "I've got my pen, pleeeease let me draw something on her door."

"No!" replied Maya. "Too obvious. I've got a better idea."

The door opposite Ms Kotka's bedroom had no name plate, just a picture of a shower. Poking her head around the door cautiously, Maya found the room empty and slipped inside. It was a small shower room with cold white tiles under her feet and a grey toilet in the corner. Like the corridor outside it was illuminated from the ceiling by a harsh, bright light.

Maya hastened to the far corner of the room where a grey plastic toilet roll cover was mounted on the wall. She patiently pulled all the paper off the large roll inside except for a single sheet, which she left hanging down from the cover so it looked like there was plenty inside.

"That should make for an awkward start to another day of tormenting children," she thought to herself, before turning her attention to the sink and shower.

Above the sink was a small cabinet with a mirrored door. Opening it, Maya saw an assortment of tubes, bottles and cosmetics, each bearing a set of initials in permanent marker. "I guess a group of teachers must share this bathroom," she mused, rummaging through the contents. "Ah, this should work – hair remover. It says 'CdM', I'm guessing Professor De Molle uses it on her legs. Now if I can just add a little to this bottle of shampoo marked 'IK'…."

Moments later she re-joined Ella and Jessie in the corridor. "Let's move on," she suggested, after explaining what she had done. "It's too risky staying on this floor."

Jessie and Ella agreed, and they headed back to the dark stairwell to make their way onwards.

JESSIE'S TV DEBUT

The next two floors were largely disappointing. Each was in darkness, and contained a series of almost identical classrooms similar to those they had already used for some of their lessons.

They made their way through each classroom, looking for anything out of the ordinary, but it was a fruitless search. Jessie couldn't resist drawing a large heart on one of the blackboards with the inscription "IK and Doctor S 4 ever xxx" underneath.

"Don't look at me like that, Ella," she pleaded, seeing a worried frown on her friend's face, "They won't know it was us, any of the children could have drawn it."

"Except that most of the children don't write in English," Ella pointed out. However, such was their disappointment at not finding anything else of interest that even Ella was happy enough to leave the heart on the board, almost as a protest.

Eventually they reached the last classroom at the western end of the second storey, which had wide, bare windows on three sides. Before them on the other side of the glass, clearly visible despite the darkness of night, stood the laboratory building next to the school house. It was impossible to see inside the building because its windows had an opaque, frosted coating, but there was no mistaking the light that blazed from each of them, spilling out onto the frozen ground surrounding the building and making its metallic walls glimmer.

The girls stood and looked at the strange building for a minute before Maya spoke. "Wow, Dr Stoker is going to get a big electricity bill - either he's on a great tariff and doesn't care, or there are a lot of people still working in that building."

"What kind of scientists work at 1AM?" asked Ella, glancing at her watch.

"Evil ones, I'm guessing," suggested Jessie with a nervous giggle. "Are we going to try to get in there?"

Maya considered this question for a while. The sleek exterior of the building suggested there would be no easy ways in, no windows left open or fire escapes left ajar that they could slip through. Additionally, the roof of the lab bristled with security cameras trained on every possible angle of approach – far more than even the ultra-secure school had.

Then there was the question of whether they even *wanted* to get inside. Adelina's description suggested it would be very dangerous to do so; maybe even that having got in they might never be able to get out again! This seemed to echo the warning that Katia had hidden in her bag. Then again, the strange boy in St Petersburg had said, "You have to find a way in". Was he talking about the mysterious laboratory? But even if he was, what did he expect her to achieve once within its forbidding walls? And would it make sense to put herself and her friends in danger based on the request of a complete stranger?

"Not tonight," she answered at length, "we need to find out more about it from the other children, and work out a plan. We won't get anywhere if we just try to barge in there. According to old smirky-chops Stoker we're going to be here for weeks, so we can wait for the right moment. Let's go and take a look around the ground floor here instead."

"Are you sure Maya?" Ella cautioned her. "We know they have security people on the front desk down there, and they work late – remember it was late when we arrived, and there were still four of them on duty."

"We can handle a few dopey security guards," urged Jessie, "I say we go and take a look around."

"There are a couple of other reasons for going downstairs," Maya added. "First of all, that's where all the computer rooms are. We might be able to get online and email our families, to make sure they know we don't like it here and want to come home as soon as we can. Secondly, the front desk is the only place I've seen any phones since we've been here, apart from Stoker's office. If we can't email home, we can try calling."

Ella had to accept these were persuasive points. All three of them were feeling incredibly homesick considering they had only been away two nights, and the thought of somehow contacting their families filled them with new hope.

Retracing their steps back to the stairs, they quietly descended to the ground floor. The found the main corridor deserted, but brightly lit like the teachers' floor they had seen earlier.

"I bet that means people are still up and about," whispered Ella. "We have to be careful."

They passed several empty classrooms, heading in the general direction of the front desk. The ground floor had more cameras than those above, forcing the girls to take several detours to avoid them. As they cut through the science block, Jessie peered through the door of the room where their memorable lesson had taken place that afternoon, then beckoned the others over.

"Look at that, Ella," she hissed excitedly, "Looks like your script did its job!"

Through a glass panel in the door they could see nine or ten men and women in white lab coats gathered around one of the computers that attached to the strange helmets the children had worn. The computer had been partially dismantled, and bits of it were all over the desk and spilling onto the floor. The adults looked tired and irritable, with their shirts as crumpled as their hair, as they read manuals and checked information on their tablets. One bald man, who looked as though he had lost the will to live, was listlessly banging a keyboard with a hammer.

"They must have been sent over from the lab to fix your little virus," Maya guessed. "Looks like they've been at it all night and I don't think they're getting very far! I don't think any of the children will be getting their brains rattled by those machines tomorrow."

Ella gave a modest smile, and pulled her friends away from the door, "That's great, but let's carry on while they're tied up in there. Maybe the entrance hall will be empty and we can try those phones you saw."

Maya nodded agreement, and they hurried along the passage to the double doors that led to the school's grand main entrance. Peeping through, they were disappointed to see two of the security officers who had been working on the evening they arrived at Taymira: the young, rather scruffy looking guard, and his towering, beefy companion.

They were sitting close beside each other writing something, and seemed quite intent on their work. Behind them, dozens of monitors in neat rows on the wall showed the feed from each of the cameras the girls had dodged on their way down from the dormitory. The second monitor on the top row was blank, which Maya assumed was because it was showing the inside of her black sock, still fastened in place over the camera at the top of the back stairs.

"OK, I've got another slightly dangerous idea," Maya informed her friends. "I'll go and attract their attention on one of those monitors, and when they come to find me, you can nip in and call home."

"No Maya," Jessie objected, "you can't have all the fun. It's my turn to do the risky bit this time; you can help Ella call our families."

After a brief debate, the plan was agreed. "Just promise me that once you've got their attention, you'll disappear back up to the dorm and pretend to be asleep," Ella pleaded. "Don't let them catch you."

"Don't worry about me, shipmates," replied Jessie with a wink. "They won't see me for dust." She gave them a cheerful salute and slipped away back down the corridor.

"She'll be OK, you know how fast she is," Maya reassured Ella, and they turned back to look at the displays behind the two guards. They caught a fleeting glimpse of Jessie moving from screen to screen as she passed each camera on the ground floor, but the security men remained engrossed in their writing and paid her no attention.

Eventually they saw Jessie stop under the camera next to the back stairs. She had obviously decided this would be the best place to make her escape from, because she now started jumping up and down and waving her arms in an attempt to attract the notice of the guards.

"It's not working," Ella whispered nervously, "They aren't seeing her."

Jessie was now putting her gymnastics skills to good use, cartwheeling across the screen, walking on her hands and generally putting on a real exhibition, which was sadly wasted on the infuriatingly unobservant guards. When she stopped occasionally to listen for any noise of people approaching, Maya could see she was getting a little frustrated. Finally, she misjudged a hand spring and hit a large metal cabinet on her landing. There was a resounding crash, which echoed through the silent school like an explosion. The larger of the two men put up a hand to catch his colleague's attention, and they both turned to the screens behind them to find the source of the noise. After a moment they spotted Jessie gingerly picking herself up off the floor, and quickly rose to leave.

Maya and Ella flattened themselves against the wall behind the door and held their breath as the two men came out of the entrance hall and made their way quickly down the passage. As soon as they had gone past, the girls slipped into the hall and quietly closed the door behind them. Maya exhaled a long sigh of relief; they were in!

PASSWORD PERMUTATIONS

Maya and Ella headed straight for the reception desk vacated by the security guards, upon which were the things they desperately wanted: a row of computers and two telephones.

Ella sat in front of one of the computers, an expensive looking silver laptop which was chained to the desk. "It's locked," she said, "we'll have to guess the password. It says the User ID is 'Snake', which is weird."

"How can we guess it?" asked Maya. "It could be anything."

"I'll try the most popular options," Ella explained. "Lots of people use really obvious passwords because otherwise they forget them."

She tried several options.

"*password*... no."

"*password123*... no."

"*qwertyuiop*... no."

"*zxcvbnm*... no."

"Why would that be popular?" asked Maya.

"It's just the bottom row of keys on the keyboard. OK, I really need to think now, if we try too many we'll get locked out."

"Maybe it's the same as the user ID," Maya suggested. "That would be easy to remember."

"OK, good thinking... let's try *snake*... no... how about *snake01*... no."

"Wait!" Maya interrupted suddenly. "I think I might have it – try *BumWeasel*."

"Errr, okay... trying *BumWeasel*... no good. What on earth made you think it was that?"

"Just messing with you, sorry."

"Well stop messing with me and make yourself useful," Ella demanded. "We don't have much time. Have a look around on the desk – sometimes people write down their passwords and leave them near their computer."

There wasn't much clutter on the desk, but Maya picked up the notepad they had seen the guards writing on.

"Hah, they weren't working at all," she told Ella. "They were playing hangman. Looks like one of them has just lost, but he got almost every letter."

The pad showed a badly drawn stickman complete with a gibbet and rope, and underneath were the letters –

G E E _ E R

Ella glanced at the pad before turning back to the computer. "Don't know what that is, Maya, probably some Russian word. Have a look and see if you can find any whole words written in there."

"Hang on…," Maya replied, "it's a long shot, but try *geezer*."

"OK, trying *geezer*… doesn't like that, I'll try *geezer01*… whoa!"

The login screen suddenly disappeared and was replaced by the computer's main menu.

"We're in! You're amazing, Maya."

"Well, don't thank me, thank the genius who used his password as a hangman clue. Maybe it's his favourite word. Quickly then, open a web browser and let's send some emails."

There were no obvious options for starting a web browser on the menu, but Ella's fingers flew across the keyboard typing commands and within seconds a browser window opened.

However, after a moment's hesitation it displayed an error message saying, "No Internet connection."

"Argh!" Ella yelped in frustration. "Who has a computer with no Internet connection?"

"People with something to hide?"

"OK… maybe there's some way I can get around it, I just need some time."

But it seemed time was the one thing they didn't have, because at that moment the double doors from the school corridor flew open with a crash and a stranger's voice shouted "Oi! What the hell's goin' on in 'ere?"

STRANGERS IN THE NIGHT

The two guards stood in the doorway, blocking their escape. Maya's eyes flew to the outside door on the other side of the entrance hall, but she could see it was bolted; there was no way they could make it over there and get the door open before the two men caught them.

"Well?" the younger of the two demanded. "What's your game? Come to steal our laptops or murder us to death in our beds, 'ave you? Well, you reckoned without the Snake, didn't you?"

Saying these words, the guard adopted a martial arts fighting posture, as if braced for imminent attack.

Maya could hear her heart pounding in her ears, making it difficult to think straight as she tried to come up with a way to get them out of trouble. Nothing came to mind and the silence started to become uncomfortable, so in the end she just started talking in the hope that the right words would somehow fall into place.

"What happened was, I woke up in the middle of the night and needed the bathroom – do you ever get that? – and I tried to use the one on the top floor but the door wouldn't open, so I got my friend to come down to the third floor with me and try the teachers' bathroom, but would you believe someone had used all the toilet paper? So then we came down here and my friend was a bit nervous about creeping around the school at this time of night but I said 'Don't worry, this school has really amazing security people, we'll be completely safe' and then we heard this loud crashing noise from somewhere so we came here to tell you about it but there was nobody here. So… then we decided to see if you had any good games on your computer while we waited. And then you came back. And now here we all are."

The younger guard listened to this speech with great attention, nodding in agreement when Maya praised the school's security team. Suddenly it seemed to dawn on him that he was dealing with two little girls from upstairs rather than an organised criminal gang who had broken in on his watch, and he visibly relaxed. Realising that he was still crouched in a defensive karate position, he straightened up and elbowed his silent colleague playfully in the ribs.

"See, just a couple of the kids from upstairs, I don't know what you were getting in such a panic for," he admonished the tall, muscular security man, who wore a slight frown but no other immediately obvious signs of giving way to panic. "Girls, you were bang on: there's nothing to worry about when we're on patrol, you are in safe hands."

He sauntered over with a jaunty swagger, and flopped into one of the two vacant chairs next to the girls, beckoning his lumbering companion to do the same.

Extending a hand for Maya to shake, he continued, "Sidney Sissinghurst is the name girls, but people call me the Snake. It's coz I'm cool, and a little dangerous when I need to be, if you know what I mean. Do you know what I mean?"

"Oh yes, definitely know what you mean," Maya agreed enthusiastically, relieved to find that they weren't being immediately marched to Dr Stoker's office for questioning. "Are you sure people don't call you 'Snake' because your name has the letter 'S' so many times – so it sounds a bit like the hiss of a snake?"

The young man's face seemed to cloud with doubt for just a moment as he considered this question but his worried look was soon replaced with an optimistic grin. "No, I'm pretty sure it's the cool and dangerous thing, like I said. What are your names?"

"I'm Maya and this is Ella."

"OK, yeah, cool, cool. One of the teachers told us that we should look out for three new girls who might be lookin' to cause a bit of bother, but there's only two of you, so I guess it ain't you, right?"

"Exactly," replied Maya with a smile. "As you say, there are only two of us, so the teacher must have meant someone else. We'll be sure to let you know if we do see three children causing any trouble though."

"Thanks Maya," her new friend replied. "I'm basically in charge of security around here, so nothing gets past me. I mean, don't ask the teachers who's in charge of security coz they might say someone else, but it's basically me."

Maya was keen to humour the young man and keep him in a convivial mood. "Wow, okay. You're doing really well to be in charge of all these guards when you're still quite young."

"Well, yeah. I mean, I am seventeen and a half. But yeah – doing well, doing really well."

"So I'm guessing from your accent you must be English – how did you end up in Siberia?"

"Yeah – Siberia! Mad, yeah? Born and bred on the mean streets of Basingstoke I was. Basically, I was a legend back home: I nearly had a recording contract coz I was one of the top rappers in Hampshire, and I was pretty certain of having trials with Chelsea too. Thing is, Mum wanted me to get a bit of experience of real life before I became a big celebrity, so she had a word with Uncle Lesley, and bosh! Here I am."

"Uncle Lesley?"

"Yeah, that's it – Lesley Stoker. He's my uncle. He's in charge of this whole gaff, you know. Well, I say he's in charge, but he kind of relies on me. We basically run the place together. I do the security, and he does, you know, whatever."

Reading between the lines, Maya imagined Dr Stoker might have been pressured by his sister to find a use for his otherwise unemployable nephew and had stuck him on the graveyard security shift where he wouldn't get in the way too much. However, she saw the value in not hurting the guard's feelings, so she nodded understandingly while he spoke, and tried to look impressed when he exaggerated his own im-portance.

"So, Sidney…" she began to reply, only to be interrupted.

"Hey, Maya, we're mates now. Call me The Snake. Or The Snakester. Or Snakey-Wakey. No, actually forget that last one, sounds a bit weird."

"OK, Snake," Maya resumed, "so who's your friend here?"

"This guy?" Snake jerked a thumb towards his thick-set companion, who had taken the seat beside him but still hadn't spoken, and was regarding the girls with an inscrutable, blank expression. "His name's Vladimir, but I call him Vladders. He really respects me, follows me everywhere, thinks I'm a total legend – and let's face it girls, he's not wrong!"

"OK, so together you are… Snake and Vladders?" cut in Ella.

"Yeah, that's what I said, try to keep up luv." Snake rolled his eyes and whispered to Maya, "Is your friend a bit slow on the uptake? She seems to think our names are funny, or something."

"No, no, nothing funny about those names," Maya hastened to reassure him. "Vladders is very quiet, does he speak English?"

"Only a few words," explained Snake. "I've been teaching him new ones by playin' hangman with him but he's not getting it very quickly. So far he only knows *Snake, Legend, Awesome, Cool* and *Geezer*. He keeps trying though; it's because he looks up to me, yeah? He wants to understand every word I say."

The idea of the enormous Russian looking up to his rather undersized English colleague was faintly ridiculous, but again Maya took care not to betray any sign of amusement and turned the conversation gently in the direction that would serve her purposes. "I bet you're a real computer genius aren't you Mr Snake? You probably even know how to get online on these laptops don't you?"

"Sorry luv, not bein' picky or anything, but it's just 'Snake', yeah? 'Mr Snake' sounds a bit like a children's TV character. But yeah - I know my way around a keyboard. Thing is, my uncle has this place on complete lock down, coz of all the important science malarkey we've got goin' on. There is no way at all to get on the web from this place; I've tried, believe me. Back home, I'm a bit of a legend – did I mention that? – and I've got a lot of people who want to know what's happening with me, yeah? People love to see pictures of the Snake: where I'm at, what I'm doing, who I'm doing it with, you get me?"

"Yes, I can imagine."

"Course you can Maya, you're a sharp kid. You get that a guy like me is gonna be in demand. Since I've been here though, I've not been able to send one message or post one picture. I recorded a new rap yesterday, now I've got no way of uploading it. Do you want it hear it?"

"I'd love to, but maybe another day, when I can really take the time to listen to it properly."

"Cool, cool, yeah, no problem, cool," Snake replied, affecting a casual air. "Another day – cool."

"Perhaps you could help me with something else though," Maya prompted him quickly, to deflect from his disappointment over the lost opportunity to share his rap. "I really want to call home, to tell my family how awesome it is here and about the really cool people I've met."

"Oh right, cool people, yeah? Like…?"

"Well, there's you obviously; just between the two of us I think you're a bit of a legend."

"Well, I dunno where you got that idea," Snake replied modestly, while glowing with pride at the compliment, "but I suppose, yeah, some people would say I'm pretty cool, yeah. Thing is though, kid, calling home is a bit of a problem. There are a lot of people in the Basingstoke area who would love a call from the Snake, especially the ladies, yeah? Can't be done though – Uncle Lesley has it set up so that you can't make international calls from anywhere in this building, and as for mobiles – we're in the middle of nowhere ain't we, so that's a non-starter too: no signal."

"Oh," said Maya dejectedly, "so you can only call Russian numbers? That's no good to us."

"Hang on Maya, how about if we call someone here in Russia but ask them to email our parents," suggested Ella, who had been playing hangman with Vladders, teaching him the words "Escape" and "Freedom".

"Great idea," enthused Maya, "except… they probably won't speak English, so how will we be able to ask them to help us? Do you know any Russian, Snake?"

"I've picked up a few words," the young man replied. "I'm one of those people who can just nail pretty much anything with hardly any practice, so I can probably help you out."

"OK, great; how would I say 'Please help me, I need to ask a favour'?"

"Right, yeah, errr, let me think for a sec. 'Please help me'…
I think that would be *Mne ochen' zhal'*… and then the other bit
would be *ya presledoval tvoyu kuritsu.*

"OK, so *Mne ochen' zhal', ya presledoval tvoyu kuritsu.*"
Maya practised it a few times. The phrase didn't exactly roll
off the tongue.

"Hey Vladders!" she called over to the Russian guard, who
was looking at some more English words Ella had given him
as homework. "*Mne ochen' zhal', ya presledoval tvoyu kuritsu.*"

Vladders looked a little surprised, but raised a hand as if to
say, "No problem."

"Right, I'm going for it," Maya decided. Picking up one of
the telephones, she dialled numbers at random until she heard
a ring tone. The phone rang for what seemed an eternity, perhaps not surprisingly at that time of night. Eventually, a man's
voice answered gruffly "*Zdravstvuyte?*"

Maya suddenly wished she hadn't called, but having got
this far decided to see it through. "*Mne ochen' zhal', ya presledoval tvoyu kuritsu,*" she stammered, a little shakily.

There was a brief pause, and then the man began shouting
a stream of incomprehensible Russian at her. Maya couldn't

understand a single word, but there was no mistaking that the man was angry. She hung up quickly and turned to Snake. "He seemed cross," she informed her new friend, "any idea why?"

"Well, I'm thinkin' two things. Number one, you've called a random stranger at nearly two o'clock in the morning. Second thing, now I think about it, I might have told you to say 'I'm really sorry I chased your chicken'."

"Chased your chicken? What kind of lunatic calls someone in the middle of the night to apologise for chasing a chicken? You made me sound like I was completely mad, or drunk, or both!" Maya complained a little petulantly. However, seeing Snake's face fall she couldn't stay angry with him. "Well, you were only trying to help," she relented, "I think we just need to plan more carefully before trying that again."

"What are all these screens for?" asked Ella, who had been listening to their conversation. Of course the girls knew perfectly well what the screens were for, having spent most of the night dodging the cameras they were connected to, but they also now knew that their new acquaintance liked nothing better than talking about himself and his "important" position on the security team.

"This lot?" replied Snake, brightening up immediately. "This is the nerve centre, kid. Nobody moves in this school without me knowin' about it, yeah? I've got eyes everywhere... look."

He began pointing at the screens, describing each one in turn.

"That one's the dining hall... main corridor on the ground floor... maths block... science block. We've got some techies working in there tonight on a computer problem, but it's all very complicated, nothing you two would understand."

Maya suppressed a smile and winked at Ella over Snake's shoulder as he continued, "Then we've got the classrooms upstairs, teachers' corridor, girls' dorm, boys' dorm... hey, that's strange: this one should show the back staircase, but it's gone blank."

He was looking at the feed from the camera that the girls had blocked earlier that night with Maya's sock.

"Don't worry girls, you're still safe," Snake reassured them. "We'll go and check that out in a minute and get it back up and running."

"That's a relief," Maya replied, making a mental note to get her sock back as soon as they could. "What about the lab next door, do you have cameras in there?"

"Oh yeah, course!" Snake assured her. "My uncle's doing amazing stuff in there, saving the world using science an' all that. We can't have just anyone wandering in there upsetting the applecart, so he needs me to keep a close eye on it. Look," he explained, pointing out some more screens, "there's the front door... back door... east wall... west wall... roof... we've got it all covered."

"What about the inside, though?" Maya asked, trying to keep her tone light and casual and not give away her great interest in what lay within the imposing scientific research facility. "Do you have cameras showing what's going on in there that we could see?"

"Sorry luv, 'fraid not. That building has its own security command centre, just like this only even bigger, I reckon."

"You reckon? Haven't you seen it?"

"Funny thing is, me and Vladders have never been in that building... Uncle Lesley thinks our skills are best used over here, keeping the students safe, yeah?"

"Oh, okay. Makes sense."

"Listen girls, not bein' funny, but isn't it time you went back up to bed? Our shift's nearly over, and the guys who come to take over might not be quite as cool as we are. They're always sayin' stuff like 'Uphold the rules at all times', and 'Do not speak to the student resources', and 'Stop getting yoghurt on the keyboard'. Total killjoys, yeah?"

Snake glanced nervously at the wall clock as he said these words, and Maya realised that for all his talk of being in charge he would probably be in as much trouble as the girls if any of the other adults found them there at such a late hour.

"Yes, I understand. Come on, Ella, let's go. Pleasure to meet you, Snake, and you too Vladders," she called, and the two of them made their way quickly back up the dark stairs to their cold beds.

DORMITORY DEBRIEF

When Maya and Ella had retrieved the incriminating sock and finally arrived back in the girls' dormitory, Jessie was lying awake waiting for them.

"You've been *forever*!" she exclaimed as soon as they were safely back in their beds. "What happened? I thought you must have been caught and hauled straight off to the lab. I was giving it ten more minutes, then I was going to arm myself to the teeth and come after you on a rescue mission, all guns blazing!"

"Arm yourself with what, dear Jessie, just out of interest?" asked Ella, amused at the thought of their small but determined friend single-handedly storming the heavily guarded laboratory.

"Oh, I don't know…" Jessie replied, as she quickly scanned nearby objects looking for suitable weaponry. "This book could give someone a nasty paper-cut… plus I've got some scissors and I'm not afraid to run with them."

"Well, thank goodness for everyone involved you weren't forced to put that excellent plan into practice," Ella concluded.

"Yeah! So – tell me all about it: what happened? Did you manage to speak to our families? Did you get caught? Why were you so long?"

Maya and Ella did their best to answer these and many more questions that occurred to Jessie as they told the story of their meeting with the two guards, their failure to make contact with home, and the secrecy surrounding the lab.

Jessie was a little despondent when they had finished. "I was really hoping you might be able to call my parents," she admitted. "I can't take six weeks in this miserable place, we need someone to come and pick us up, and soon. So did we learn anything useful at all?"

"Well, I guess we know a few things," Maya replied thoughtfully. "Dr Stoker seems to have gone to great lengths to cut this place off from the outside world. He has to be hiding something, and something serious at that: you don't go to this much trouble just to hide the fact that you're serving your students a bad flavour of jelly at lunch time. Having said that, we've searched the school pretty thoroughly without finding anything more suspicious than the strange equipment they use in their science classes. I think we can be pretty sure that whatever secrets this place holds lie firmly within the metal walls of the building next door."

"It's funny Snake and Vladders haven't been allowed in there, isn't it?" mused Ella.

"Well, Snake isn't the sharpest pencil in the case, but I don't think he's a bad person. His uncle wouldn't want him wandering around in the lab if they're doing something naughty in there; he certainly isn't the type to keep his mouth shut."

"That reminds me of the other useful thing you found out," said Jessie with a gleeful chuckle, "Dr Stoker's first name – Lesley! It quite suits him…"

Tired after their long night's work, the girls agreed it was time to sleep, and resolved to make more plans the next day. For a few minutes Maya could hear Jessie quietly repeating "Dr *Lesley* Stoker" and giggling, but soon she was surrounded by nothing but gentle snores.

Turning on her side so she could gaze out of the tall window next to her bunk, Maya saw it was a clear night and looked up at the stars. They shone much brighter here than back home in

England, and the sky seemed to twinkle with twice as many lights as she had ever noticed before.

"Are you up there, Mum and Dad?" she wondered. "What would you want me to do? Stay out of trouble and wait for six weeks until Dr Stoker lets us go? Or would you want me to find out what's happening here? You taught me to question anything I didn't understand... but you both gave your lives looking for answers. You wouldn't want me to put myself in danger – but maybe it's even more dangerous to do nothing!"

Maya found herself going over and over the same points, unable to rest. Eventually she grasped her snowflake necklace in her hand and made a conscious effort to clear her mind. Moments later the darkness of sleep closed around her and bore her away to a land where she could fly away like a bird, leaving the school far below her.

CRIME AND PUNISHMENT

The harsh buzzing noise from Maya's bedside screen was even more unwelcome the next morning than it had been on their first day, loudly intruding on her dreams only four hours after they got back to bed.

The other girls in the dorm followed their usual routine, quickly and silently dressing and making their beds. The only difference Maya noticed was that Adelina was not there, which seemed odd given that she had been in her bed when they went to sleep.

Ella was sitting up in bed and gave Maya a sleepy wave as she swung her legs over the side of her bunk and climbed down the ladder. Jessie, who could sleep though an earthquake, was still fast asleep in her bottom bunk so Maya gave her a gentle shake, followed by a less gentle shake, followed by a tweaked nose. This did the trick, and a few minutes later the three of them had wearily struggled into their uniforms.

"I can't be bothered to mess around with putting our hair in stupid buns this morning," announced Jessie, crankily. "My hair is a free spirit like me – it wants to float around and do its own thing."

"Actually Jessie, I'm with you," Maya agreed. "We've already broken about a thousand rules, I'm sure one more won't hurt. Ella?"

"Well, we don't want to upset the teachers needlessly... but then again, my hair doesn't follow orders even when I want it to," Ella replied, ruefully flicking a golden curl out of her eyes. "Let's just go with pony tails like I had yesterday."

They agreed on this point, and when they joined the line of children standing stiffly to attention at the end of their beds they did so with three defiant pony tails flowing down their backs.

Ms Kotka came for her morning inspection just as she had the previous day, although this time she wore a black head-scarf over her dark grey hair. Maya's heart raced at the thought that their teacher must have used the shampoo she had mixed with hair remover during their adventures last night. It had seemed a good idea at the time, but how would Ms Kotka react; would she guess Maya was involved?

The tall, gaunt figure made her way down the line of girls a little quicker than usual, spitting a word of criticism here and there but in truth paying little attention to the assembled children. She marched down to the end of the room where Maya waited nervously, and for a moment their gazes locked. Maya was trying desperately to look the teacher in the face and not allow her eyes to wander up to that headscarf, searching for signs of what lay beneath. A moment under the icy stare was all she could bear before looking down at the thin carpet, but she felt Ms Kotka's cold eyes continue to rest on her.

An uncomfortable pause of several seconds followed, and eventually Maya risked another peek at her adversary. What she saw was even scarier than she expected, for the teacher's face was now twisted into a leering smile of spiteful pleasure. She anticipated a cold reprimand of some kind, or perhaps to find her name going into the dreaded notebook, but was surprised to see the teacher turn on her heel and stalk back down the row of children and out of the room.

"What do you think that was about?" asked Ella. "Do you think she had that scarf on because of the hair remover?"

"Of course she does!" Jessie chimed in. "She is one crazy bald baboon under that scarf – and she obviously doesn't know it was us or she would have said something."

"Hmmm, I hope you're right, Jessie," Maya said thoughtfully. "I just didn't like the way she was smiling. As a general rule, things that make Ms Kotka smile are not likely to be good news for us."

They made their way down to breakfast in the dining hall, where they were delighted to be given burnt toast with a meagre scraping of butter. "This is the nicest food we've had since we've been here, things are looking up!" Jessie announced cheerfully. During breakfast Adelina came into the hall, but to Maya's surprise she sat on her own in a far corner rather than joining them.

Shortly afterwards Ms Kotka entered the room, her hawk-like eyes scanning the rows of benches as she prowled the hall's central aisle. "I hope she's not looking for us," Ella whispered, and the three girls found themselves instinctively hunching forward over their food to be as unnoticeable as possible. Inevitably though, the teacher's penetrating gaze soon alighted upon them and she called sharply, "Maya Madison, Ella Kelley, Jessie Bell! You will come with me."

Once again the girls found themselves being led downstairs, past the main entrance and along the corridor towards the double doors of Dr Stoker's grand office. The principal was at his desk, drinking a black coffee and reading something on his laptop.

"Girls!" Stoker exclaimed when Ms Kotka presented them to him. "Girls, girls, girls..." he leant back in his chair, shaking his head and chuckling ruefully. A silence followed, with both adults clearly taking pleasure from keeping the children in suspense.

Maya waited patiently, certain they were in trouble but ready to issue denials or make excuses depending on what the principal accused them of.

Eventually Dr Stoker leant forward and continued. "I know what it's like to be a little girl, and want to have adventures, and mess around, and have fun... don't forget I was one myself, once."

"You were a little girl?" asked Maya, quizzically.

"No, I mean I was a child... a boy, obviously!"

Dr Stoker's puffy cheeks flushed a little redder than usual in embarrassment, but he blustered on. "Now then, girls – you probably think you're very clever, but you need to understand that I'm a little bit cleverer; I know exactly what you got up to last night."

"Last night?" Maya echoed, looking upwards and wrinkling her lightly freckled nose as if trying to cast her mind back to the previous evening. "Nothing's coming to mind... did we forget to brush our teeth?"

"Hah!" interjected Ms Kotka from behind them. "Do not try the Director's patience, insolent child!"

Stoker raised a hand to calm his sour-faced employee, and leant back in his seat again with his hands behind his head, confident he had the upper hand. "There's no point in lying, Maya. As I said: we know what you did last night. You may as well be honest about it."

Maya thought quickly. Back at Crinkleton she had often found that it paid to own up and apologise when you had no chance of wriggling out of trouble, because you might then be punished less severely. This was different though – Dr Stoker was nothing like the well-meaning teachers back home. He had lied to them several times already, so why should honesty impress him?

The other problem was that she had no idea how much he really knew – did he know they went exploring? About the toilet paper and the hair remover? About the blocked camera, or their attempts to get online, or the failed phone call? Did he know they had been asking about the lab next door, and were still planning to find a way in there to uncover whatever dark secrets he was so anxious to hide?

Trying to coax some more information out of Dr Stoker, Maya began, "Oh! So you know about…"

"Yes!" the Academy Director cut in, exactly as Maya had hoped. "Thanks to one of the other resources – I mean, one of the other children - I know you left the dormitory last night! And I know exactly where you went."

"Oh," replied Maya in a small voice. "You know about that do you?"

"Yes," Stoker assured her, "I know all about that!" He was beaming with smug contentment now at this illustration of his knowledge and power. "You went down to the upper class-rooms and you drew something quite ridiculous on one of the blackboards."

Maya's eyes widened in surprise – Jessie's silly heart graffiti! If that was all he knew about it was a lucky escape, so she tried to look as disappointed as possible. "Yes, well… we're sorry, okay? We were just a bit homesick so we went for a wander and messed around a little bit. No real harm done, surely?"

"Girls, in my school children do not go for wanders, nor do they mess around. And to draw something on the board suggesting any romantic involvement between me and Ms Kotka... well, it's absurd, and quite disgusting."

Maya longed to turn around and see if their teacher found the idea quite as unpleasant as the Principal claimed he did, but to avoid making the situation worse she simply hung her head and stared at the floor, waiting for him to continue.

"Your punishment will be twofold: firstly, you will spend the whole day shredding old paperwork for me. Secondly, you will be denied use of the telephone for the next eight weeks."

"Eight weeks?" Jessie queried in surprise. "But you said we would only be here for six weeks."

"I'm pretty sure I said six to eight weeks," Stoker replied complacently. "Now go – Ms Kotka will take you to the back office so you can get started on that shredding."

The adults exchanged a rather awkward parting nod before Ms Kotka turned and strode quickly from the room with the girls following dejectedly behind her.

LOLA

Ms Kotka led the girls down a side passage to a small, windowless room with metal filing cabinets along three of the four walls. In the centre of the room were a big laser printer, a shredder and a pile of empty sacks.

"Another student will bring some documents for you to shred," they were informed. "Put paper in here, press green button, simple. You will not do anything else, you will not play games or mess around. You will shred everything that is brought to you. At the end of the day I will inform you when you can leave." The teacher kept distractedly patting her headscarf as she delivered these curt instructions, and departed swiftly afterwards, closing the door behind her.

The three friends looked at each other, each wondering how the others would react to this latest downturn in their fortunes. Maya spoke first.

"Have to say it, Jessie – this is another fine mess you've got us into. I wish you hadn't drawn that heart."

"Whoa, it's not all my fault! We all agreed to go exploring at night, and we always knew there was a chance we would get caught."

"Come on you two," interrupted Ella, soothingly, "we can't turn on each other. We need to stick together to get through this. And you know – it might actually be a good thing they found the heart and blamed us for it."

"How could it be a good thing?" asked Maya in surprise.

"Well, they seem to think the only reason we were out of bed was to draw silly pictures on blackboards. If it wasn't for that, they might dig a little deeper and find out about everything else we've been up to. If they guessed we've been trying to contact home, and wanting to find out what they're doing in their creepy lab, we would probably be stuck in this room forever!"

Maya saw Ella's point, and put an arm around Jessie. "I'm sorry, okay? You're right, nobody was keener than me to go on last night's jaunt, and I'm glad we did. And as Ella said, it could be a lot worse."

"No problem, Double M," replied Jessie, who liked to give her friends new nicknames whenever the fancy took her. "You know what I'm wondering though – who told nasty old Kotka about our little escapade?"

"I hate to say it," Maya replied, "but I think there's a good chance it was Adelina."

Ella slowly nodded agreement, but Jessie's face fell. "Adelina?" she asked in amazement. "But she's our friend! We helped get her out of trouble yesterday morning, and she knows about Ella's awesome work in shutting down the science class for the next day or two. Why would she tell on us? It was probably one of the boys."

"They're in a separate dorm, they couldn't possibly have seen us unless they were out of bed too – and they would be crazy to admit that to a teacher. Think about it: I know Adelina saw us leave the dorm. Then, she wasn't around when we were getting dressed and when we went down to breakfast. And when she did come into the hall, she didn't even look at us; she probably felt too guilty."

Jessie listened to Maya's arguments, her expression gradually changing from disbelief to anger.

"Yeah, I bet you're right!" she concluded. "She must have got up before six and gone straight to one of the teachers to tell them what she saw. Well! When we see her again I'm going to… to…" Looking around for inspiration, Jessie grabbed some blank sheets of paper lying on the printer.

"I'm going to destroy her!" (tearing the paper). "I'm going to pulverise her!" (crumpling the paper into a big ball). "I'm going to drop an elbow on her!" (approaching the printer with the intention of demonstrating a wrestling move)

Maya and Ella swiftly stepped in to prevent a potentially disastrous girl-versus-printer conflict, and sought to calm their impetuous friend.

"Dear Jessie, you know perfectly well you wouldn't hurt a fly and you have no intention of doing any of those things," Ella began.

"No," Maya added, "and don't forget we don't know for sure whether it was Adelina. She's been nicer to us than anyone else here, so it would be surprising for her to turn against us now. We'll find out what happened before we do anything too hasty."

Jessie's emotions could change like the wind, and she immediately passed from enraged to rather downcast as Maya said these words. "You're right," she agreed, "it's not like we have a lot of friends here, we can't afford to lose Adelina if it turns out it wasn't her."

Looking around them, the girls began to wonder if the filing cabinets contained anything of interest. Trying to open a few they found them to be locked, and were just starting to work their way around the room checking each one when a voice said from the doorway, "Locked – they're always locked up, tighter than a crocodile's jaws, he he!"

The three friends span around in surprise, and saw a girl a little younger than themselves standing in the doorway. The girl had a broad, infectious smile and long, thick curly brown hair that was in the process of escaping from the regulation Taymira bun. She was carrying a large pile of paper in front of her, with her chin resting on top.

"Hello, is that the paper we have to shred?" asked Maya.

"This is your first pile," the newcomer explained, "I've got many more to bring you, don't worry, don't you worry now." With these words she crossed the room and placed the paper on the floor before hoisting herself on top of the printer and then sitting there swinging her legs, quite at her ease.

Maya watched her in surprise, having grown quite used to the sombre and downcast expressions of the other children at

Taymira. The little girl began whistling a tune, but cut off abruptly to say, "I'm Lola, although some of the children call me Loopy Lola, I'm not sure why, he he! I know who you are though: Maya, Ella and Jessie, yes? My friend pointed you out in the dining hall yesterday – the new girls from England, come to stay with us forever, hah hah!"

"Nice to meet you, Lola," Maya replied. "I think your friend made a mistake though – we aren't here forever, just for a few weeks."

"Sure, a few weeks, which turns into a few months, and then a few years, and then you are just like me – here forever!"

Maya glanced nervously at her friends, who she could see were torn between doubting the eccentric girl's prediction and believing the worst because her words matched their deepest fears – being stranded at Taymira indefinitely.

"How long have you been here, Lola?" Jessie enquired.

"How long?" the girl echoed, and then repeated to herself, "How long has Lola been here in the dark place? As long as she can remember, as long as a river, sparkling in the sun."

"Well… OK, let's start with this: how old are you?" asked Maya.

"Oh, I don't know, I lose count of the days… I'm pretty sure I'm not old though, I don't need a walking stick or anything like that. I think I'm a child, just like you, he he!"

"Yes, you're certainly a child," said Maya, encouragingly, "but don't you remember your last birthday? How many candles were on your cake?"

"Ah, Maya, there are no birthdays here. My friend told me all about them, with games like pin-the-parcel, peel-the-tail-off-the-monkey, and hide-and-sleep. I like how it sounds… but there are no birthdays for Lola, he he…"

Although the little girl finished this sentence with her usual giggle it had a very sad ring in Maya's ears.

"What about before you came here?" she asked. "Do you remember how old you were when you came?"

"I don't remember anything before coming here, I think I was too young. Sometimes Professor De Molle gets me to pour her glasses of her special grape juice, and then usually she gets angry or sleepy, but one time it turned her all nice and friendly to me. Then she told me some things about before Lola came here: she said she found me in an orphanage in a far-away land called Nigeria, when I was not much more than a baby… she said she offered to take me to a lovely private school and give me a good start in life, and the orphanage people were very happy and said she could. I think she might have told them the school was a bit nicer than it really is, he he!"

"Yes, I bet she did," agreed Maya. "So are you in the class below ours? I haven't seen you with them in the so-called 'recreation area', when they line up to go to their next lesson."

"No, I am not really in the class anymore," Lola replied. "I used to be, when I was much younger. In fact, I think I was the best at science, because I was always the first to be chosen for new experiments. But then I started to go a bit wrong, and get muddled up. That's why they call me Loopy Lola, because I get a bit confused with things, and then I wasn't allowed to be in the experiments anymore, or the other classes. I still remember a bit of the learning though: one plus 'A' is cat, the capital of maths is noun... or something like that. Knock, knock!"

As she said these words, the little girl rapped her knuckles on the side of her head as if to help arrange things in her mind, before giving them a beaming smile and continuing. "Yes, no more lessons for Lola, no no. Now I just do little jobs for the teachers, like bringing this paper for you, or cleaning the fireplace, or making their drinks. If I'm good, I can stay here, and

I won't be sent to live in the cold forest out there." She gestured vaguely beyond the walls of the windowless room.

"What, so they're treating you as a servant, and threatening to let you freeze to death outside if you misbehave?" asked Jessie in a tone of outrage.

Lola looked a bit startled at Jessie's anger, and pulled her knees up in front of her so she could sit with her arms round her legs and hug them. "You don't understand, I must have said it wrong, I always do that. I'm lucky to be here, really. It's much warmer than outside."

Maya put up a hand to warn Jessie not to upset their visitor, and asked, "How come we haven't seen you in the dorm? I thought every girl in the school slept there?"

"Oh, I used to have a lovely bed there." Lola explained. "That was my favourite time of day: bed time, he he! Getting under those covers and snuggling around until you got warm… one time another girl gave me a bracelet she had made out of little bits and pieces she had found, it was beautiful, and I kept it under my pillow. It's gone now though. I can't sleep there any more, I think maybe because I had nightmares, and woke up the other children…"

Lola's voice trailed off and she stared at the ceiling as if trying to remember something. "Oh yes!" she suddenly added after a pause, holding out her arms. "There's this as well, look: my skin is this funny brown colour, not the usual proper colour like yours – so I think it's best if I'm on my own."

Maya looked at her friends in horror. They had seen and heard some unpleasant things in their time at Taymira but this was a new low.

"Lola, listen to me, there is nothing wrong with your skin," she said reassuringly, moving over to the printer and taking the little girl's hand. "You know, back in Nigeria most people have skin just like yours, there's no such thing as a 'normal colour' or 'proper colour'... I can't believe nobody told you that."

"But some of the teachers don't like it..."

"Some of the teachers are idiots then," Maya concluded firmly. "I happen to know that Professor De Molle uses fake tan to try to make her skin darker, I bet she didn't mention that! Don't let them tell you there is anything wrong with you, you are just as you should be. So where do you sleep? Where's your bedroom?"

"My bedroom? Hah hah! This is my bedroom, you are all my guests, he he! In fact, you are standing on my bed."

Maya looked down and saw she was standing on one of the sacks that was piled up next to the printer. "You sleep here?" she asked incredulously. "Don't you even have a bed?"

"It's okay, my sacks are quite soft," Lola assured her, "and I still get to have my meals with the other children, they still remember me, they won't forget Lola, he he!"

"Don't you ever think about escaping from this horrible school?" asked Ella.

"Escaping?" Lola looked quite surprised at the idea. "Where would I go? My friend told me it's a long way back to Nigeria. And if I got there, what would I do then? I don't know the name of my orphanage, I don't even know what town or city I come from. I might be out of the frying pan and into the kettle. No Maya, I'll stay here, here forever."

With these words Lola nimbly dismounted from the printer and skipped merrily out of the room. "Got to go now," she called over her shoulder as she left, "but I'll be back in two sticks."

A SHRED OF EVIDENCE

The encounter with Lola left Maya momentarily speechless as she turned to her two friends. It didn't have the same effect on Jessie who strode to the nearest metal filing cabinet and began kicking it. "I – *(bang)* – HATE – *(bang)* – THIS – *(bang)* –SCHOOL!" she shouted, before running out of energy and slumping against the now dented cabinet.

"Okay, Jessie, take it easy," Ella pleaded, "we know how you feel though. Just when you think these horrible teachers and scientists can't get any worse it turns out they're racists as well."

"It's not just that," Jessie replied mournfully, "it's everything they've done to her: experimenting on her since she was a toddler, and then shoving her away down here out of the way once they'd messed up her brain so she can't think straight. We have to get her out of here."

"Like she said though," said Maya thoughtfully, "she doesn't have parents to go back to like you two, or a family like mine. I don't know where she would go. Still – every problem has a solution; I'm sure we can find a way to help her."

While discussing this point they had begun to look through the papers Lola had brought them. Maya was hoping there might be some interesting information amongst the hundreds of sheets in the pile, but to their disappointment they found that every single document was in Russian. There was nothing for it but to proceed with the tedious task they had been assigned, feeding the pages into the shredder a few at a time. Unlike the shredders Maya had seen before which cut the pages into strips, this machine cut and sliced the paper so finely it became almost like powdery white snow, which collected in a big bucket at the bottom.

An hour later they were all done, and soon enough Lola came back with more paper for them.

"Hello, hello, English friends!" she greeted them. "Wait, can I call you my friends?"

"Yes, of course."

"And how do you like my other friend, Mr Shreddy?" she asked, giving the shredder an affectionate pat.

"Erm, yes, he's lovely, probably one of my top five favourite shredders of all time," Maya replied. "Lola, isn't there ever any paperwork in English?"

"Oh yes, Dr Stoker has lots of English letters, but he's a clever man, very clever, he he! He gives those to children who can't read English, and he gives you the Russian ones. And to carry them around, he gets the girl who can't read at all!" Lola jerked a thumb towards herself with a smile.

"Well, that's only because these useless teachers haven't taught you properly," Maya told her. "Do you think there is any way you could bring us some of the English documents next time?"

"Can I bring you English papers? I *can* bring you English papers!" Lola ran from the room without another word, and soon returned with a new pile of paperwork, this time in English as promised. Maya and her friends grabbed handfuls of them eagerly and began reading through them.

"We might find something useful in all this," she said to the others. "We might as well have a good look through – we've got all day."

It was clear that Dr Stoker didn't like reading on his laptop, because he had printed out all kinds of things. Jessie flipped through a few of the documents, calling out their titles: *"A Study of the Effects of Helium upon the Common Toad"*, *"Proposals for the Weaponisation of Flatulence"*, and *"Dairy Allergies, Humanity's Greatest Challenge"*.

"Look at this," said Ella, showing them one of the first pages she looked at. "It's an email to an artist, looks like he's getting his portrait painted, listen: 'Please try to capture all my most obvious qualities – my intelligence, bravery and heroism – but don't neglect my compassionate, caring, handsome side'... yuck! It tells us one interesting thing though..."

"What, that he's smug, deluded creep?" asked Jessie. "We knew that already."

"No, Ella's right," Maya corrected her, "it tells us he has access to email – perhaps the school isn't quite as cut off from the outside world as he likes everyone to think."

"Here's another one where he's nominating himself for a Nobel Prize," Ella continued. "... in the light of my significant advances in the treatment of itchy buttocks, and of course my charitable mission to help educate needy children from all over the world..."

"Hah! His 'prize' for that should be a slap around his wobbly chops and ten years in jail," Jessie replied with a mirthless laugh. "Is there a reply?"

"Yes," Ella read on with a faint smile, "We are sorry to inform you that your discoveries in the field of posterior relief, while impressive, do not have the capacity to change the world for the better... I bet he didn't like that! So is that what they're doing next door, making bum cream?"

"I have a feeling he's up to more than that," Maya replied. "He's obviously desperate for fame and glory. He's probably trying out all sorts of things. I think... wait a minute, look at this!"

She spread a handful of pages over the floor and the three girls knelt in front of them, scanning through them quickly. Maya's eye had been caught by the mention of Crinkleton, the home that they had left just two days ago but now seemed a lifetime away. The pages turned out to be a long exchange of emails between Dr Stoker and their headmaster at Crinkleton, Mr Sneed. They were dated a few weeks ago, and started with Dr Stoker proposing an exchange of students "to promote international co-operation and understanding".

"Oh look," Ella exclaimed in surprise, "Mr Sneed suggested sending Oscar." Oscar was one of the best students in their class, clever and hard-working, with a gift for languages. "Well, I know he isn't exactly a barrel of laughs, but I can see why Mr Sneed would pick him... Dr Stoker said 'no' though."

Sure enough, Dr Stoker had written back to say that he wanted to send Katia to Crinkleton, so it would be better if the student coming to Taymira was a girl too. Then Mr Sneed had proposed sending Emily-Jane, another of the brightest and best behaved children at Crinkleton - but this time Stoker had rejected her on the basis of her age. "We have a preponderance of children born late in the school year, so the ideal candidate to match our pupils' level of development would be somebody born in mid-August," he had written.

"That seems ridiculously picky," Ella commented, "but look – that's when Mr Sneed suggested you two."

Perhaps tiring of having each child he suggested turned down, Mr Sneed had offered Stoker a choice of having either Maya or Jessie visit his school, pointing out that both their birthdays were in August and providing a range of samples of their school work to help the Taymira Principal decide. The next email showed that just two minutes later Dr Stoker had made his selection, choosing Maya and asking for her to be sent as soon as possible. A few days later when Mr Sneed checked if Jessie and Ella could come too, the reply was just as rapid: "Allow the dear child to bring whomever she wishes, provided this does not delay her swift arrival."

Maya's first reaction was one of indignation. "I can't believe Mr Sneed didn't pick me first – I was third choice!"

"Oh, come on, Maya!" Ella chided her. "Put yourself in his shoes – Oscar is the captain of the chess club; you got banned from chess club for inventing the 'fireball defence'. At the science fair, Emily-Jane created a box camera; you created an explosion that broke three windows and nearly killed a goat. Who would you pick?"

"I didn't nearly kill it, it was just a bit startled – but I take your point," Maya conceded. "I suppose the more worrying point is: it almost looks like Dr Stoker set out specifically to bring me here, out of all the children at Crinkleton."

"How do you work that out?" asked Jessie.

"Well... first he insists on a girl, then it has to be somebody born in August, which limits it straight down to you and me. Then when Mr Sneed sent our work for him to look at he didn't even bother – he just picked me right away. And when Mr

Sneed asked about you two coming with me – suddenly he didn't care about age any more: he didn't even ask how old Ella is."

"But why on earth would someone you've never met go to all this trouble to single you out and fly you halfway around the world, only to immediately start being mean to you and giving you stupid punishments?" Jessie inquired. "I think you're imagining it Maya – he wanted a girl who was at the younger end of the year because he was sending a similar girl over to Crinkleton, simple as that."

"Is anything simple around here though?" asked Maya. "Let's keep looking through this paperwork."

The next email was to a publisher. Dr Stoker wanted to know if they would be interested in printing his life story, entitled *Becoming Amazing – How I Used My Genius for the Good of Mankind.* "They've kept the reply short and sweet though," chuckled Ella. "It just says 'Thanks, but no'."

"OK, this one is to the lovely Ms Kotka, but it's just boring science stuff." said Jessie, passing a page to Maya with disdain.

"It's not boring, Jessie," Maya replied with a patient smile. "Let's have a quick look…" Reading the message through,

Maya saw it was dated a few days previously, when Ms Kotka had been at Crinkleton with Katia. "It's strange though," she told the others, "he's telling her to administer a large amount of Ferric Nitrate to someone. I'm surprised you would ever give someone this much deliberately – it causes stomach pain and vomiting."

"She was probably force feeding it to poor Katia, just for fun," Jessie suggested with a scowl.

"She didn't seem ill, though," mused Ella. "We didn't get the chance to talk to her very much, but I think we would have known if she was in pain."

"You know who was ill around about that time though," Maya reminded them, "Miss Acres! Don't forget she was supposed to be bringing us here and staying for a few days to help us settle in, but she got sick at the last moment. It does make sense: Stoker and friends wouldn't want an adult coming here and asking awkward questions. There's no way Miss Acres would let them treat us like this, she'd have taken us straight home again."

They looked at each other in silence for a moment. Could there really be some sort of bizarre conspiracy to get them to Taymira and keep them there?

"Have to say, Jessie, I think she might be right," said Ella at length. "I'm starting to think Dr Stoker did single out Maya to bring over, and now he wants to keep her here. The only question is: why?"

TAO

The rest of the day provided the girls with no more information of interest. The remaining paperwork was concerned with boring administrative matters, so eventually they went back to their original task of shredding it.

By the time the huge piles of paper had been dispatched it was nearing the end of the school day. Opening up the shredder, Maya saw that the bucket collecting the finely shredded paper powder was nearly full. "I might just borrow some of this," she told her friends, scooping some big handfuls into her pockets.

Moments later, Ms Kotka appeared. "Well girls, I hope you have learned your lesson – there will be no more sneaking around at night, no?"

"No, Ms Kotka," the girls chorused, although they had already agreed they would wait a couple of nights and then begin exploring again.

They were released from the stuffy back office and made their way back towards the school's main corridor. Noticing Dr Stoker's car parked outside, Maya beckoned her friends to follow and led them out into the courtyard, and then through an archway to the small parking area at the front of the school. It was already dark, providing plenty of cover as they crept around to the far side of the car and crouched down.

"I'm nervous, Maya – what are we doing?" asked Ella.

"Are we going to puncture his tyres?" suggested Jessie. "I hope so!"

"Something much more fun," replied Maya with a wink, and reaching into her pockets she began to stuff handfuls of the tiny shreds of paper into the air intake vents at the front of the principal's car.

"Oh, they're like thousands of little snowflakes… but what will that do?" asked Jessie. "Stop his air-con from working?"

"Difficult to describe," Maya explained, mysteriously, "you'll just have to wait and see."

When they got back to their dormitory Adelina was there, reading a book. Feeling Jessie tense up beside her and wanting to avoid a confrontation, Maya asked her tempestuous friend to go and watch Stoker's car through the window on the landing while they spoke to their Finnish classmate.

As she approached Adelina with Ella, the tall, slender girl turned her pale face towards them with a look that showed both a guilty conscience but also a quiet resolve. Without any prompting, she closed her book and said calmly, "I told Ms Kotka you left the dormitory last night. I know you can never forgive me. You must do whatever you think is right: shout at me, or call me bad names, or even strike me, I will understand."

Seeing the deep sorrow in Adelina's blue eyes, Maya immediately knew that no reproaches were necessary: she was already punishing herself quite enough. "We're not going to yell at you," she said gently, "but why did you do that? You must have known we would get in trouble for it... I thought we were friends?"

"Yes," Adelina replied earnestly, "and your friendship means a lot to me, but there is one thing that means even more – my brother, Tao. Remember I told you he was taken to the lab? Well, that was many weeks ago and he never came back. Ms Kotka came to me yesterday evening, and told me that if I watched you and told her about any bad things you did then she would tell me what had happened to him."

"It might be hard for you to understand, but Tao is all the family I have in the world – I just had to know. So, when I saw you leave the dormitory last night I knew I had to tell Ms Kotka. I hated myself for doing it but I felt like I had no choice. I could have told her much more: about how you put slime in Dr Stokers briefcase, or how you broke the computers in the science class room, or many other things… but I wanted to say as little as possible so you would not get in too much trouble."

Maya and Ella exchanged a look of understanding. Ella had an older sister, so Maya could easily imagine her in the same position. However much she valued her friends, Maya knew Ella would do almost anything to help her sister if she was in some sort of danger – so how much more strongly must Adelina feel, with no parents and no other family to support her?

She put an arm around the Finnish girl and asked, "So what did old Ms K tell you once she had the information about us? Was it worth it?"

Adelina's shoulder sagged as she replied, "She told me my brother died a few weeks ago, trying to escape. And then she laughed." Her eyes filled with tears and she buried her face in her hands, sobbing silently.

Maya and Ella comforted her as well as they could, although there were few words they could find that would offer any consolation. Their classmate had lost the only light that shone into her bleak and hopeless future, and now found herself completely alone. What could anyone say that would make her feel better?

Showing a lot of inner strength however, after half an hour had passed Adelina dried her eyes and asked about the punishment Maya and her friends had been given. Maya told her everything, knowing that there was no way their trust would be betrayed again. They talked about Lola, about the documents they had found, and their fears that she had been hand-picked to come to Taymira for reasons they could not guess. Then Maya asked if Adelina knew why Dr Stoker would be so keen to keep his visitors at Taymira.

Adelina glanced around before replying, and lowered her voice. "This is not a normal school, Maya. Children are sent here from all over the world, and very few ever leave. When my friend Katia was sent to your country I told her that she must take her moment to escape. There are many orphans here, or children with parents who will not ask questions about them."

"Oh!" said Maya, "Well, I'm an orphan, but Jessie and Ella aren't. I'm sure their parents will be really worried if they don't hear from us soon, and so will my aunt and uncle. Don't you have any other family at all, Adelina?"

Her new friend cast her eyes down sadly. "I don't think so – it was always just me and Tao, as long as I can remember. I can't believe I will never see him again."

"That's awful," said Maya, giving Adelina another hug, "You must miss him so much."

"Yes, he is a good brother, he makes it bearable here… or at least he did." Adelina replied, and reaching under her bed pulled out a photograph from her case. "This is Tao, the last picture I have."

Maya looked at the picture in surprise. It showed a younger Adelina on a wooden swing, hanging from the branches of a tall tree. Adelina was laughing, which Maya had never seen her do, and pushing the swing was a boy – a boy she had seen once before!

"Adelina," she exclaimed, "Your brother isn't dead: I saw him two days ago!"

She waved Ella over and explained, "We saw him at the airport in St Petersburg. He warned us to be careful about coming here. Look, Ella... it's him, isn't it?"

Ella looked closely at the picture and agreed, "Yes, I'm pretty certain."

Adelina gripped their hands so hard it hurt, and begged them to take one more look. "Please – look again, be sure! If you're right, this is the happiest moment of my life!"

Ella and Maya studied the photo again. Even without the hat he had been wearing at the airport, they felt there could no mistake. "It was Tao, I'm sure of it," Maya confirmed. "He even had the same accent as you. That old hag was lying to you – probably bitter because Tao really did escape somehow."

Believing them at last Adeline put her face back in her hands and wept again, not silently this time but loudly, unable to contain the tears of joy that streamed down her face. Then she wrapped Maya and Ella in her long, slender arms and locked them in a tight embrace, wordlessly expressing her gratitude for the new hope they had given her.

When she finally collected her thoughts and dried her eyes once again, she wondered how on earth Tao could have made his way to St Petersburg. "It's thousands of miles away, and he has no money," she explained.

"He also said he had met your parents, Maya," Ella reminded her. "What can he have meant by that?"

"Yes, that was really odd," Maya agreed. "My parents have been lost for so many years, I don't see how he could ever have known them. And he said he had seen a picture of me, too."

They looked to Adelina for an explanation, but she could offer none. "When we came here Tao told me Dr Stoker was the first English person he ever met, and he wondered if all English people were evil," Adelina explained, "so he can't have met your parents, can he? But, I am so happy that he has escaped from the lab somehow. This is the happiest news you could have given me!"

Just then Jessie rushed into the dorm, her dark, wavy hair flying out behind her. "Quick, quick!" she called to Maya and Ella, waving frantically and hopping from one foot to the other in her impatience. "Our beloved principal is heading for his car!"

They hurried back out to the landing and sat on the stone window ledge, which offered a great view of the small parking area at the front of the school. Dr Stoker was just getting into his black jeep, five storeys below them.

"What happens now?" asked Jessie. "Please tell me the car explodes…"

"Just wait, be patient…" Maya scolded her, as they pressed their noses to the glass. Dr Stoker started the car, and for a moment nothing happened – then an instant later the Jeep's interior was filled with a thousand tiny fragments of paper, sucked in through the air vents. The paper swirled around, kept aloft by the jets of air from the car's heating system.

"Awesome!" whispered Jessie in hushed appreciation. "It looks just like a snow globe in there!"

All three of them got the giggles as they watched Dr Stoker first sitting motionless in shock as the in-car snow storm raged around him, then flapping his arms around wildly in an attempt to disperse the paper flakes. Finally he started hammering the controls on his dashboard, and after turning every light on, sounding his horn and setting off his alarm he finally managed to switch off the heating, allowing the paper to settle around him.

"He's getting out!" Ella warned. "Duck down so he doesn't see us!"

Ella and Jessie dived for cover below the window ledge, but something made Maya stay put. She watched as Stoker rubbed his short grey hair, sending a shower of paper in every direction, then turned to look at the school – his gaze seeking out the windows around the girls' dormitory.

Maya folded her arms and resisted the temptation to hide, and a moment later their eyes met. They scowled at each other for what felt like an eternity to Maya, although it may only have been seconds. A look passed between them which seemed to say, "I will get the better of you," before Stoker turned on his heel and stamped back into the school, slamming the outer door behind him.

"Are you crazy, Maya?" asked Ella.

"Yeah, I'm with Captain Cautious on this one," agreed Jessie. "Don't you think he'll know it was you?"

"Oh, I don't know, you're probably right," Maya confessed as they headed back into the dorm. "I guess I just wanted him to know I wasn't scared of him."

"Maybe you should be though," Ella replied ruefully. "He seems to hold all the cards at the moment."

Adelina spent the rest of the evening asking them for every detail they could remember of the few moments they had spent with Tao. Maya went to bed that night feeling more confused than ever. Why had Tao come to find her at the airport? Could he really have met her parents? Had Dr Stoker singled her out to bring to Taymira – and if so, why?

WILLOW

When Maya awoke in the morning she thought she must still be dreaming as snowflakes danced before her eyes. Then she realised that she was staring straight at the display screen next to her bed, which was showing a funny pattern, with snowflakes twinkling where there was normally just text.

Glancing at Ella's display in the next bed Maya saw that her screen just displayed the usual words, none of which she could understand except for Ella's name. "Maybe mine is faulty," she thought to herself, watching it for a few more moments. The flakes swirled back and forth across the screen, almost like they were doing a little dance, and Maya found herself fondly holding on to her snowflake necklace as she looked at them. Then, to Maya's amazement, they were replaced with a message that read "MAYA COME TO LAB". The message disappeared as quickly as it had appeared, leaving Maya blinking in surprise.

She watched the screen for a few more minutes but it had gone back to the normal display of her name with some Russian words underneath, and neither the snowflakes nor the unusual message reappeared. She told Jessie and Ella what had happened as they were having their breakfast.

"I don't know about the message, but maybe the snowflakes were some sort of weather forecast," Jessie suggested, "It snowed really heavily last night."

Sure enough, the countryside visible through the frosty windows was covered by a thick coat of fresh snow which sparkled in the weak morning sun. After their first class of the day (another dull Maths lesson in which they copied out their times tables over and over again) the girls got their coats and boots on and went outside for recreation time. "I'm not surprised they don't call it 'Play Time'," said Ella. "Nobody ever seems to play anything around here."

Sure enough, most of the other children were simply standing around shivering or talking quietly to each other. "Too scared of getting in trouble and being sent to the lab," Maya replied. "I'm certainly not going there just because some silly screen tells me to – when we go it will be on our own terms, without anyone else knowing. Let's go and play hide and seek down by those trees."

The school field was bordered at the back by a large pine forest, which stretched off into the hills as far as the eye could see. The girls ran across to where it began and Ella said, "OK, I'll count to twenty. Don't go too far in though, or I'll never find you!"

She started counting and Maya and Jessie scurried away in different directions, looking for a good place to hide. Maya chose a tree whose lowest branches dipped all the way down to the ground, forming a thick canopy that blocked most of the light. "Ella will never find me in here," she thought to herself with a smile. Ella's voice came floating through the trees as she searched, muffled by the snowy branches, and Maya could tell she had gone to look in the direction Jessie had taken.

Peeping out from her hiding place a few minutes later, Maya noticed in dismay her own footprints in the fresh snow leading straight up to the tree she was hiding under. "Oh dear," she thought, "if Ella thinks of following our tracks she'll find me in no time!" She was just thinking about trying to cover them up somehow when she noticed another set of tracks leading up to her tree.

The tracks were smaller than hers and quite rounded, and had made very little impact on the snow. "I can't see any tracks leading away," Maya thought to herself, "I wonder if there could be a little creature in here somewhere?" She looked around in the gloom, and her eye fell on a pile of leaves near the tree trunk. She crept towards it as quietly as she could and gently brushed the leaves aside, then gasped in surprise. Blinking nervously up at her was a baby white wolf!

Maya froze with amazement for a moment, then rushed back outside the cover of her tree and called for Ella and Jessie. Her two friends appeared together a moment later. "You're not very good at hide and seek, Maya," teased Ella. "You're supposed to stay quiet when you're hiding. What's happened?"

Rather than reply, Maya waved them to follow her through the thick tangle of branches to the base of the tree. The little whelp was still there, looking tired and lonely. "It's a wolf, a baby girl!" Jessie exclaimed, and they knelt down to gently stroke it.

"She must have got separated from her pack," said Ella, "I'm pretty sure a wolf this young shouldn't be left on her own."

"What can we do to help her?" Maya wondered.

"Let's take her back to school and hide her somewhere so we can look after her," suggested Jessie.

"Yes, let's!" the others agreed.

"When she's a bit bigger and stronger she might be able to find her pack again," said Maya hopefully. "If we are going to look after her we need to give her a name. How about Willow?"

Her friends agreed, and Ella wrapped Willow up in her scarf. "Now Willow," Maya coaxed her fondly, "you're going to have to be very quiet when we sneak you into the school. We don't want any of those nasty teachers getting their hands on you!"

No sooner had Maya spoken than a dark shadow fell across them, and the protective branches of the tree were thrust aside. "Well, girls... and what do you have here?" asked the voice they least wanted to hear, and before them stood the imposing figure of Ms Kotka.

A DARING RESCUE

"We are always grateful for the chance to help young animals in our Scientific Research Institute," Ms Kotka informed them with a cold smile, and before they could move she reached down and snatched the little white wolf from Ella's arms. "Come now! It is time for your next lesson."

With those words she turned and marched back through the woods to the school field. The girls looked at each other in horror. Whatever was going on in the labs next door to the school, they were quite sure it wasn't going to be a nice experience for Willow.

"Nobody hurts baby wolves on my watch, we have to get her back!" whispered Maya, and her friends nodded agreement. They raced after their teacher, and then followed her at a distance so they could see where she went. They watched from behind a wall as Ms Kotka went inside a low outbuilding behind the school, then come back out moments later without

Willow, issuing some rapid instructions to somebody using her mobile phone.

After waiting a few moments for Ms Kotka to walk away towards her classroom the girls crept inside the outbuilding. It looked a bit like a stable, with a rough stone floor and bare brick walls, and contained little except for a cupboard, a row of cages along the back wall, and a lingering smell of manure.

Each of the large cages stood open and empty except for the last. Maya's heart jumped for joy as she saw Willow huddled miserably in one of its dark corners. They ran to the cage and found that it was bolted but not locked. Sliding back the bolt, Maya reached in and gently picked up Willow, who gave her a friendly lick of gratitude.

"Now what do we do?" she asked her friends.

"I don't think we can keep her here at school," replied Jessie. "Ms Kotka will look everywhere for her, I bet."

"We have to find her pack," said Ella. "It might be dangerous but I think it's the only way we can save her."

"Let's go back to where we found her and try to follow her tracks back to the pack," suggested Maya. "We need to hurry though! I bet someone will come looking for Willow soon, and they will be wondering why we aren't in class."

They rushed back out of the building and over the field towards the forest. It didn't take long to locate the tree Maya had found Willow under, but to their dismay they saw that the tracks had disappeared under a fresh dusting of snow. "I'm pretty sure they came from that direction," said Maya, pointing deeper into the forest, so they set off.

They took it in turns to carry Willow, keeping her as warm as they could by tucking her inside their coats. Soon the trees thinned out a little, and the girls felt quite warm as the sun reflected back on them from the perfect blanket of snow beneath their feet. They seemed to walk for hours, but saw no sign of any other wolves.

As the afternoon wore on, it quickly started to get dark and then the girls began to feel the cold. They looked at each other in concern. "I'm not sure we can find our way back in the dark," said Ella, with a worried frown.

Looking behind them at the shadowy outlines of trees in the fading light, Maya agreed. "We can't stay out here though, can we?" she replied. "We'll freeze!"

Looking around them, they saw what looked like a little cave halfway up a steep hill to their left. "Let's see if we can make it up there," Jessie suggested. "At least it might be a bit warmer."

The girls struggled up the hill, quite exhausted by now. When they got to the cave they found it was small, no bigger than Maya's bedroom, but at least it was dry. They tried to start a fire by rubbing sticks together, but their numb hands could hardly hold the wood. Giving up, they huddled together for warmth with Willow in the middle and tried to sleep.

Feeling the night growing colder and colder Maya worried that they would all wake up as icicles. She lay facing the entrance of the cave, and watched as large, fluffy snowflakes began to fall from the sky again. The flakes fell slowly, almost like white feathers, merging into the thick layers of snow outside as they landed. After a while a single flake, guided by some tiny, unfelt gust of wind, separated from the others as it drifted lazily downwards and made its way inside the cave, landing just in front of Maya.

"It's just like me and Willow," she thought bleakly. "An orphan, left alone, with no family… nobody cares where it falls."

She stifled a quiet sob, feeling a moment of hopelessness. A minute later though, a dozen more snowflakes were blown in from outside, landing around the first one. Hearing the quiet snores of Ella and Jessie behind her, Maya took heart.

"You can't think like that," she told herself firmly. "You've got the two best friends in the world, an aunt and uncle who love you like a daughter, a wolf cub who needs you to help her get home, and a school full of children back there who somehow need rescuing from Stoker's clutches. I'll never be alone, I've got people who care about me..."

With her mind at peace, Maya was hit by a wave of exhaustion. As she closed her weary eyes, she felt as though a large shadow loomed over her, but she was too tired to do anything but fall into a deep sleep.

THE PACK

When Maya woke up she felt delightfully warm, and snuggled up closer to her warm, furry blanket. Then she remembered where she was and that she didn't have a blanket. Slowly opening her eyes, she saw found that she was actually snuggling up with an enormous adult wolf! The wolf had its eyes closed and seemed to be asleep. Cautiously looking around her, trying not to make a sound, she saw that they were surrounding on all sides by six or seven wolves, lying curled around the girls as they slept. Ella's head was resting on a wolf's soft white back as a pillow, while Jessie had a tail wrapped around her neck like a scarf.

Hardly daring to breathe, Maya gently tapped her two friends with her foot until they woke. Ella gave a gasp but smothered it with her hands as Maya frantically signalled to her not to wake the wolves. The girls slowly got to their feet, and Ella and Jessie crept outside the cave, leaving Maya holding Willow in the middle of the circle of wolves. Looking around, Maya saw that the wolf closest to her was a large female. She stooped down and placed Willow between her powerful front paws, whispering "I bet this is your mummy Willow… she'll take care of you now."

Willow licked the she-wolf's soft cheeks and wagged her tail happily, then lay down looking quite contented. Maya rose to slip away, but as she did so the wolf's piercing blue eyes suddenly opened. Maya froze in terror, and for a second they stared at each other, motionless. Then the mother wolf turned away and began to lick and fuss over her little cub, and Maya gratefully fled outside to where her friends were waiting.

"Let's get back to school as quickly as we can," urged Jessie, "The days are so short here; we don't want to get stuck again!"

The sun was shining again over the snowy forest as they made their journey back the way they had come. Maya told her friends about her encounter with the mother wolf. "I think they knew we helped their little girl, that's why they saved us last night. I'm sure we would have frozen solid without them."

They all agreed they had had a lucky escape, and chattered merrily as they made the long trek back to school. As they came to the edge of the forest and the old school building stood before them once again, however, they began to worry. Would they be in trouble for missing lessons? Not to mention rescuing Willow from getting sent to the lab - and what about staying out all night?

PRINCIPAL PROBLEMS

It was early afternoon when the girls arrived back in the school yard. They planned to wait a few minutes until afternoon recreation began, and then re-join their class. As they crept across the frosty concrete, however, a nearby window flew open and the face of Dr Stoker appeared. His cheerful and ingratiating tone was nowhere to be seen as he coldly commanded, "My office, now!" then slammed the window shut.

The girls looked at each other in dismay. There was nothing else they could do but gloomily make their way to the main entrance of the school and down the corridor to Dr Stoker's office. The heavy doors stood slightly open, so with a deep breath Maya opened them and they stepped inside. To their relief the Academy Director's large room was empty, although they knew trouble would be arriving soon enough.

Ella and Jessie had a look around the office, taking in the many certificates on the walls. Most of them seemed to have been presented to the Doctor in recognition of his generous contributions to various projects in the area. "He doesn't seem very generous to me," Ella commented tetchily.

Noticing that Dr Stoker's laptop was still on his desk, Maya took a quick look at what was on his screen. She was surprised to see her surname, Madison, amongst a list of other names, each with a long number against it. Glancing over her shoulder to make sure nobody was coming, Maya hit the "Print" button and the list of names slid smoothly out of the printer under the desk. She folded the page and put it in her pocket, moments before the door behind her opened.

Dr Stoker strode into the room, followed by Ms Kotka and four large men in the plain grey uniform of the school staff. "Well Maya," said Dr Stoker, "it seems you and your friends are not fitting in very well in our warm and friendly school. You have only been here for three days, and you have already broken ninety-seven school rules: failure to attend lessons, failure to report to your dormitory at bed time, inappropriate hair-styles, consorting with wolves, failure to consume re-quired dosage of nutri-slime..."

Dr Stoker's voice grew steadily louder as he listed each and every one of their offences. After a few minutes he concluded,

"… most seriously of all, inserting unapproved substances into the briefcase of a senior member of staff!"

"He found it then," Maya thought to herself. "Well, I hope his silly briefcase is ruined! It serves him right for being mean to children, and wolves."

"What do you have to say for yourself, Maya?" demanded Ms Kotka, in her usual stern voice. She was still wearing the black headscarf, from beneath which peeped a patchy wisp or two of faded grey hair.

"I should just apologise," thought Maya, "but what good will it do? We're going to have a miserable time here, whatever I say."

She looked Dr Stoker in the eye and replied, "I'm not sorry for any of it. Your school is horrid, your teachers are horrid, you're feeding the children horrid slime and making them do weird experiments. I'm glad we set that little wolf free, and if I could I'd set all the children free too! I'm sure you're going to punish me, so go ahead. Just don't punish my friends: it was all my idea."

"Very noble," mocked Dr Stoker, "but I will decide who needs to be punished. You will all be taken to our Scientific

Research Institute to assist us with our work there until further notice."

The girls looked at each other in dismay. This was the very last punishment they wanted.

"Take them away!" Dr Stoker instructed, and the uniformed men roughly pushed them out of the office and down the corridor.

"We have to get out of here!" Maya thought frantically, but she could see no escape.

THE LAB

Maya expected the men to take them out of the front entrance of the school and across the car park to the Taymira Scientific Research Institute next door, but to her surprise their guards took a sudden turn through a door further down the corridor from Dr Stoker's office, swiping a security pass to open it. Next they were taken down a steep flight of stairs.

"I didn't realise the school had a basement," Maya thought in surprise, "Where on earth are we going?"

At the bottom of the stairs the guards took them through another security door and then along a wide, brightly lit passageway with no doors or windows. "This must be some sort of underground tunnel connecting the school to the lab," Maya realised.

Reaching the other end of the passage they passed through another set of heavy doors, and found themselves in an enormous chamber whose walls rose nearly a hundred feet above their heads to the very top of the building. Before them they could see six levels of white rooms with large windows, with metal walkways and lifts allowing access to each floor. They were escorted across the chamber, allowing Maya to look into each of the rooms on the lowest level as they passed.

The rooms were clearly laboratories. Most were illuminated with an array of bright spotlights, and Maya could see people in white coats using various complicated looking machines for their experiments. In one, two women seemed to be inserting an enormous thermometer into a grapefruit. In the next, an elderly scientist was frantically pursuing a badger around the room with a net in one hand and what looked like a tiny egg-whisk in the other. In the last room they passed Maya's heart sank as she saw a child from the school being led into the lab by two grey-uniformed guards like the ones who were accompanying her. The child was a boy, a few years older than Maya, but he looked just as scared as she felt at that moment. "We'll find a way out, nobody's doing experiments on me and my friends!" she resolved.

After passing ten or twelve labs on the ground floor of the huge building they came to an elevator in the far corner of the chamber. The guards waved them inside and then followed, pressing a button marked "U3" and swiping their security pass again. To Maya's surprise the lift moved rapidly downwards. "We're going even deeper underground," she thought, "I wonder how far down this creepy building goes?"

Eventually the doors opened on a very different view from the one above. Here the lights were not bright but dull and gloomy, and the ceiling was not far above their heads but so low that the taller guards had to stoop as they walked. Maya amused herself by asking the leading guard a question just as they came to an even lower archway. Turning to answer her, the guard walked straight into the metallic frame of the archway with a resounding clang that knocked his hat off and left him sprawling on the floor. Maya giggled and thought to herself, "If he was the only guard we could make a run for it," but she knew they had no chance of escaping the three other men, especially in such a confined space. She was surprised to see Jessie help the guard to his feet, but decided her friend must be trying to befriend their captors so they would be better treated during their long stay at the lab.

After several twists and turns they arrived outside a metal sliding door. It had a small glass panel at the top, much too high for Maya to see through. The leading guard, still rubbing his sore head, swiped his card and the door slid open. The girls were ushered in, and the door closed behind them, locking with a resounding "thunk!"

REUNITED

Looking around, Maya saw that they were in what could only be described as a cell, with no windows and no furniture apart from six single beds, each with a bedside table. The walls and the floor beneath her feet were cold, unpainted stone. Sitting cross-legged on a bed in the far corner and talking quietly to two grown-ups was a girl she recognised.

"Adelina!" Maya rushed over and threw her arms around her slender Finnish friend. "What on earth are you doing here?"

"When you went missing I was questioned," Adelina explained. "When I could not tell them where you were I was sent here as a punishment."

"I'm so sorry, we never meant for that to happen, I know how scared you were of coming here." Maya felt tears welling in her eyes at the thought of causing further suffering for the unfortunate girl.

"Please do not worry about me," Adelina comforted her, "I am learning to be brave just like you. Now, you must dry your eyes, because there are people here who have waited a long time to see you."

Maya turned and looked for the first time at the man and woman seated behind her on the bed next to Adelina's. The man was thin, with messy brown hair and deep laughter lines around his eyes. The lady next to him was tall with rosy cheeks, freckles and blonde hair tied up behind her head. They were staring at her as if they had seen a ghost, and Maya felt as though she had seen them somewhere before. Then they opened their arms and lifted Maya off the floor in a tight embrace, and a burst of a hundred memories seemed to flood Maya's mind in a single moment: her mum, tying yellow bows in her hair; her dad, finding a ladybird in the garden and gently holding it out for her to see; the three of them in a rowing boat on the river, getting stuck under a weeping willow; and dozens more simple childhood scenes from when she was just three years old.

"Mum? Dad?" she asked in disbelief. "Is it really you?"

"It's really us... and it's really you! Our little Maya, so big now! How you've grown.... and you're as beautiful as the day we last saw you." Her mother sat back down on the bed and pulled Maya close to her once again, tears of joy shining in her eyes.

"We never gave up hope that one day we would see you again," her father said, wiping his eyes and kissing the top of Maya's head. "All these years we've thought of you every day, it's been the one thing keeping us going."

Looking up at her dad, Maya noticed a familiar shape hanging from a cord around his neck. She reached inside her school shirt and pulled out her snowflake necklace, holding the silver design out in front of her. Her parents smiled and each did the same, the three necklaces joining together to make an intricate snowflake. "We bought these at Christmas when you were three," Maya's Mum explained, "One piece for each of us. I never thought you would still have it."

"I looked at it every day before bed, and imagined the two of you watching over me," Maya explained. "But please tell me, where have you been? Surely you haven't been here in this awful lab for all these years? Why didn't you write to me, or call?"

"Yes, all these years we have been prisoners here," her father replied. "During our expedition to the Arctic we discovered a strange moss that had unusual properties. We thought it could be very important for use in medicines to help fight all sorts of illnesses, and we came to the nearest laboratory for help in studying it further. Dr Stoker welcomed us here with open arms but when he realised the potential of what we had found, he had us locked away so he could keep the moss for himself. Without our skills though, he couldn't unlock its secrets. He tried to force us to work for him but we refused. That's when he threatened to send someone to England to harm you if we didn't help."

Maya's eyes were wide with astonishment. Her mother continued the story. "To keep you safe, we helped Dr Stoker. We worked for many years, and started to find ways to turn the moss into effective medicines. That's when Dr Stoker began asking us to test the medicines on children. He sent children here from the school, pretending it was a punishment for bad behaviour. He then forced them to take pills and have injections, and monitored the outcome. At first the results were good, but he kept increasing the dosage. When Adelina's brother Tao was sent here the Doctor made him take pills every day for weeks, in bigger and bigger doses. We were worried the pills would kill him, and we couldn't let that happen, so we found a way to help him escape through the ventilation shaft in the lab. We would have gone too, but it was too narrow for us. We gave Tao our bank details so he could get enough money to escape back to Finland."

She turned and squeezed Adelina's hand. "Your brother is a brave boy," she told the little girl. "He said he would find a way to come back for you."

"When Dr Stoker found out what we had done," Maya's father told her, "he was furious. He said that we were not taking his threats to harm you seriously enough, so he had found a way to bring you here. We hacked into the lab's computer network and found it was true, that you really had been brought here. We couldn't email anyone for help because Dr Stoker keeps the facility isolated from the Internet to protect his secrets, but we could access the dormitory display screens. We tried to send you a message, but we were terrified somebody else would see it."

"I did see it!" Maya told them, "I had almost made up my mind to come and investigate what was going on here, but then we got thrown in here anyway for rescuing a wolf before I had the chance!"

She related the story of their adventures since they had arrived. "It was very brave of you to help that wolf Maya, but really! It's so dangerous wandering around outside in this weather... we could have lost you again!" her mother scolded, and hugged her again, closer than ever.

THE GREAT ESCAPE

Maya talked to her parents for hours. They wanted to know every little thing that had happened to her since she was three, and she had lots of questions about their long captivity. She introduced them to Ella and Jessie, and her mum said how sorry she was that they had been dragged into Dr Stoker's sinister plans. "This makes me more determined than ever that we have to find a way to escape," she told them.

"Do you think we can?" asked Maya, "How could we do it? There seem to be a lot of guards here."

"After we helped Tao escape they put extra bars on all the ventilation shafts," her dad explained. "During the day we are now watched by twice as many security staff. At night most of the other scientists go home and there are fewer guards, but we are locked in this cell. Even if we got out of here, we would need to find a way through about twenty locked doors before we got outside."

"Unless we had a security pass," said Jessie with a smile, and produced a white plastic pass in a blue holder from her pocket. "I slipped it off that silly guard's shirt when he fell over."

The girls laughed, remembering the guard's look of dazed surprise as he lay on the floor. "That's brilliant Jessie," said Maya's dad. "The only problem is that this cell door doesn't open from the inside with one of those passes. The only way to override the lock is to enter a security code, and from listening to the guards doing it we know it is a ten digit number. This means there are ten billion possible codes... there's no way we can guess it."

"A ten digit number?" Maya thought to herself. "Where have I seen one of those?"

In her pocket she found the page she had printed in Dr Stoker's office. The third line down said:

Madison - 1928000122

She showed her dad. "Maya, we've been trying to get through that door for years, and you bring us the solution after being here for three days. I can see you've grown up to be a very special girl," he told her. "We mustn't delay because the code might be changed at any time, and the guard might realise he's lost his pass. This is the moment – we have to escape to-night!"

They planned their next move carefully. "The road south from here to the airport has very little traffic," Maya's mum explained. "It will be impossible for us to get a lift, and easy for us to be caught if we go that way. Instead we need to head ten miles west, across country, to the closest town. From there we can get a train to the airport. The last train leaves at 1AM - we need to get out of here as early as possible so we can catch it."

"We know that the daytime guards leave at seven o'clock in the evening, so we should try to sneak out just after them, before the night guards get properly organised."

Everyone agreed that this sounded like the best idea, and Maya's dad turned to Adelina. "It will be difficult and danger-ous for us to reach the train and get away. Dr Stoker will keep us here forever if he can, so we must try to escape. For you, it's different. In a week or two they will take you back to the school. You're welcome to come with us if you want, but the choice is yours."

Everyone looked at the Finnish girl, and she returned their gaze shyly but with determination in her eyes. "I will come with you. You helped my brother to escape and I know we can do it too if we all stay together."

"Mum," Maya asked, "what about Lola? I told you about the awful way she's been treated, isn't there some way we can save her too?"

"I understand how much you want to help her," Maya's mum replied, "but our chances of escape are slim enough as it is. If we try to get back into the school to find Lola, we're almost certain to be caught – and that won't help anyone. The best thing we can do for that poor little girl and all the other children is to get away, expose Stoker for the monster he is and get this place shut down."

Maya reluctantly accepted her mother's point. She felt sick to the pit of her stomach at the thought of leaving Lola behind, but if they attempted a rescue and got caught they would all be stuck there with no prospect of saving themselves, Lola or anyone else.

An anxious wait followed, as the time on Mrs Madison's watch slowly crept around towards 7PM. Allowing a few minutes for the guards to get changed and leave the building, they prepared to leave at exactly 7:15. Everyone crossed their fingers as Maya's mum entered the long number into the key pad next to the door. For a horrible moment nothing happened, then there was a quiet click and the door slid open. They stepped out into the corridor feeling an amazing sense of being free – but for how long?

UNCOOL DROOL

The six prisoners stole silently through the twisting underground corridors towards the lift. Fortune seemed to be on their side as they got there without meeting anybody and all squeezed inside. Maya's dad used the security pass Jessie had grabbed, and pressed a round button marked "U1", whispering, "There's an underground loading bay for deliveries on that floor, I think it's our best route out of the building. The front doors are watched by guards and cameras, so that's no good to us."

When the lift stopped they found themselves in a small chamber with a doorway opening into what looked like an enormous underground car park. Peeping through the door's narrow glass panel they saw that a wide opening, designed for trucks to fit through and secured with metal shutters, stood at the far side of the loading bay. Next to this was a small security cabin, and inside the cabin sat a uniformed guard. The guard was sitting in front of a set of security screens, with his grey peaked cap pulled down low over his eyes. After watching him for a few minutes, Mr Madison turned to the others and whispered, "I think he's asleep."

They opened the door and crept across towards the exit. The guard made no movement, and as they got closer they could see his chest rising and falling slowly and hear gentle snoring. Arriving at the metal shutters, the escapees looked around for a way of opening them. Maya's mum waved them over to the security cabin and pointed through the window. "It's there," she whispered, and they saw a big red button on the guard's desk that surely had to be for opening the thick shutters so vehicles could get in and out.

Unfortunately, the sleeping guard was leaning against the door of his cabin – there would be no way to open it without waking him. "I can fit through there," suggested Maya, pointing to a low opening between the glass and the desk on the other side of the cabin, which was clearly used to allow the delivery drivers to hand paperwork to the guards.

Her parents looked worried at the thought of putting her in more danger, but it was obvious that there was no other way to get in safely and open the gates. The opening in the glass was much too small for a grown-up to clamber through. Everyone held their breath as Maya's father lifted her up to the right level and she squeezed through the gap. The space inside was incredibly cramped, and Maya had to duck under the guard's outstretched legs and then stand right next to his slumbering face to get near the button. The guard had a thin trail of drool hanging from his chin and snaking down the front of his jacket, and Maya felt like she could smell his last three meals each time he breathed out. Reaching out, she crossed her fingers and pressed the big red button, thinking, "I hope this isn't the alarm button, or we are in big trouble."

For a moment the steel shutters made a terrible clattering sound, but then started to move smoothly upwards leaving a gap at the bottom.

"We won't be able to close it from outside," Maya's dad whispered through the glass, "so don't open it too far. This way it won't be so obvious it's been opened - we'll just have to crawl." Maya let go of the button after a couple of seconds with the gap only a foot high. She took a moment to tie the guard's shoe laces together, to slow him down when he did finally wake up, and then slid back out of the cabin and into the loading bay.

Dropping to the floor, Maya's mum rolled under the door and waved for them to follow. The others scrambled through the gap and up a steep ramp on the other side until they found themselves outside the back of the building, with a full moon shining down on them and the cold night air tickling their noses.

FRIEND OR FOE?

The little group set off as quickly as they could to the west. First they had to climb a steep hill, at the top of which was a cluster of trees. Luckily there had not been any more snow, but Maya still found herself wishing they had snowshoes as her feet sank in up to the ankles with each step.

At the top of the hill they stopped in surprise. Tucked into a small space between the tall fir trees were two tents. They were obviously in use, because a lantern hung from a low branch nearby, casting a flickering light over the anxious faces of Maya and the others.

"Whose are they?" she quietly asked her mum. "Maybe somebody who can help us?"

"They could be something to do with the lab," her mum whispered.

They paused for a moment, wondering what to do, and not a sound could be heard in the eerie silence of the night. Then the stillness was shattered by a huge shower of snow falling from one of the trees, followed by a figure that dropped to the ground right in the middle of the group below. The newcomer sprang up, looked around at their astonished faces and then leapt towards Adelina, knocking her off her feet onto the powdery snow.

The others rushed to help Adelina, but by the time they reached her they realised she was not being attacked – she was being hugged!

"Adelina, siskoni! I was worried I would never see you again. But I said I would get us out of that school, didn't I? You always believed I would, didn't you?"

They got to their feet and Maya recognised the boy who had warned her about Taymira when they were at the airport, and whose picture she had seen at school – it was Adelina's brother, Tao. He embraced Maya's parents, thanking them for helping him to escape, and then turned to Maya. "It is good to meet you again, Maya. I wanted to stop you from coming to Taymira, and tell you what had happened to your parents, but Dr Stoker's assistants followed me all the way to St Petersburg and I could not let them capture me again. I came back here to watch the school and wait for a chance to rescue my sister, but you have brought her straight to me!" He put his arm around Adelina's slim shoulders and gave her another fond squeeze.

Just then he was interrupted by Ella, who whispered, "Look! They're after us." She was pointing back towards the lab, clearly visible less than half a mile away at the bottom of the hill. The light of the moon reflecting off the snow lent a spooky glow to the countryside, against which they could see little black figures running backwards and forwards outside the lab. Worse yet, they soon saw people pointing up towards the hilltop and the trees that concealed them, and then beginning to march up towards them.

"They must be following our tracks. We have to go," said Maya's dad. "We might not be able to outrun them, but we must try."

"I think I can help with that," Tao replied, hurrying over to the furthest tent and unzipping the front panel to reveal two snow mobiles. "I thought I would need these if I found a way to get my sister out," he explained. "They are really for one person each, but maybe we can all fit somehow."

"How did you manage to get those here?" asked Maya in amazement.

"Your parents let me use their money when I escaped," Tao explained. "I rented them from the nearest town. I had to ride the first one here, then walk back and get the second one. It was very hard, but I could not give up while my sister remained trapped in that prison."

They wasted no time in dividing up, Maya's parents taking one vehicle, with Adelina between them, while Maya, Ella and Jessie clung on behind Tao on the second snowmobile. "Hold on tight!" he shouted, and with a roar the snowmobile shot forward through the trees and onwards into the night.

TRAPPED ON THE TUNDRA

Maya clung on for dear life as the snowmobile raced through the forest, bouncing over roots and skidding left and right at the last moment as tree trunks loomed in front of them. Glancing behind her she saw Jessie and Ella had their eyes closed, a wise precaution as Tao steered them under a broad pine and got both a mouthful of snow and a slap across the face from one of the low hanging branches. Rather than slowing down, the Finnish boy laughed and accelerated even more.

Just as Maya thought they were sure to have a terrible crash at any moment, the trees thinned out and they saw open country before them. Low, rolling hills, covered by a perfect blanket of snow stretched out for a couple of miles ahead, leading to the wonderful sight of lights twinkling in the distance.

"That is the town," Tao confirmed, slowing for a moment and pointing ahead. "We can be there in ten minutes, there is no way they can stop us."

The snowmobile's engine roared as he cranked it back up to full speed and they streaked forward across the hills with the other vehicle close behind. Loud as they were, Maya suddenly realised she could hear another noise in the background, a strange thumping noise that seemed to come from all around them. She looked back, and saw that her parents were doing the same, but there was nothing to be seen coming down the hill after them.

Then Maya cast her gaze a bit higher, and saw to her dismay the dark outline of a helicopter against the starry night sky. It was descending rapidly, and heading straight for them. She shook Tao's shoulder to get his attention and pointed upwards. Seeing the aircraft looming above them, he grimaced and tried to squeeze even greater speed from the snowmobile, but to no avail. The helicopter landed fifty yards in front of them, and out of it stepped Dr Stoker accompanied by two armed guards who aimed their rifles at their escaped prisoners.

Tao slammed the brakes, and Maya's dad brought his snowmobile to a halt next to them. They waited to see what Stoker would do, thinking desperately what their next move should be.

"Well, my good friends, are you leaving so soon?" Dr Stoker asked with his usual smarmy smile, crunching towards them over the snow. "I really must insist you stay a little longer. Just think of all the good we will do, working together."

"We'll do plenty of good if you let us go," Maya's mum replied angrily. "Our discovery can help cure illnesses all over the world, but you just want to use it for your own profit."

"We'll help you," Mr Madison offered, "but only if you release the children. You have no need to keep them here."

"I'm afraid the dear little children know a bit too much about our work for me to let them go," the Doctor responded. "Besides, you have nothing to fear – at our school they will receive an excellent education, and enjoy the satisfaction of knowing that they are contributing to the world of science and to *snaaaurrrrgh!*"

The end of Dr Stoker's sentence was lost as a snowball hit him in the mouth and covered his face in a shower of snow. Everyone turned to the left to see where it had come from, and there stood Maya, who had slipped off the snowmobile as Dr Stoker was talking.

"You don't care about using science to help people – all you want is to be famous for something. You're bitter and twisted because nobody wants to publish your book or make a film about your life, and you couldn't even get on *Siberia's Got Talent*! You're a pathetic, vain, selfish loser, and we're not going back to your stupid school!" she shouted, and hurled a second snowball in the doctor's direction.

This time Stoker put his hands up to block Maya's throw but the snowball glanced off his fingers and dislodged his glasses, which fell into the snow. Once again the Doctor lost his polite manner and strode angrily over to where Maya stood, grabbing her roughly by the arm and barking, "All of you, into the helicopter right now! I can see we have been too soft on these children since they arrived. Now you will learn some respect. There won't be any more…"

His voice suddenly trailed off, and he looked around nervously. The helicopter's blades had stopped turning, and the night was silent once more, except for a new noise: a low, menacing growl which came from all sides. Blinking in the dim light without his glasses, Dr Stoker's voice wavered as he asked his guards, "What's that? Do you hear something?"

The guards raised their rifles and peered out into the night. There was nothing to be seen. One of them ran to the helicopter and brought a powerful flashlight back, sweeping the beam around them in a wide circle. For a moment there was still no sign of the source of the noise, until Maya noticed the glow of several large, bright pairs of eyes reflecting the glare of the torch. Moments later the guards saw the pinpoints of light too, but before they could react a mighty howl rose from all around them and the shadowy figures of a dozen wolves sprang forward out of the gloom!

A FAVOUR RETURNED

As startled and terrified as Maya was by the wolves' sudden appearance, she could tell that Dr Stoker was even more afraid. He gave a high pitched scream of fear and pushed Maya in front of him, backing away towards the safety of the helicopter. Maya fell to the ground in the deep snow, and lay still for a moment with her eyes closed. For the first time in her life she felt completely helpless. She knew there was no way she could get up and outrun the wolves, and even if she did there were still two armed guards who might open fire on them at any moment.

She reluctantly opened her eyes to see a wolf advancing towards her, until its powerful jaws were just inches away from her. The wolf lowered its head to sniff Maya, its snout seeming to twitch in recognition. Looking into the wolf's bright blue eyes, Maya realised it was the mother she had returned Willow to early that morning. "It seems a lifetime ago now," Maya thought to herself, "I hope she remembers me."

The wolf leaned back on her strong hind legs and then launched herself forward with her teeth bared. "This is it, I'm finished!" thought Maya, but the mother wolf leapt straight over her as she lay curled up on the ground, landing several feet behind her. The wolf grabbed Dr Stoker's arm with her fangs as he stumbled towards his aircraft and dragged him to the ground. Getting to her feet Maya saw that the other wolves had ignored her friends and family and had surrounded the two guards, who had dropped their weapons in fright.

The two snow mobiles roared back into life and Mrs Madison called out "Maya, let's go! They could turn on us at any moment!"

"They won't, they're our friends…" Maya replied, but her voice was lost beneath the engine noise, the snarling of the wolves, and the cries of the petrified guards. She ran back to her friends, Ella and Jessie grabbing a hand each and pulling her back into position behind Tao.

Looking back over her shoulder as they raced away from the chaos behind them, Maya saw the guards had been cut off from their helicopter and were running back towards the forest closely followed by Dr Stoker. The seat of the doctor's trousers bore a jagged tear, through which a surprisingly bright pink pair of pants could be seen.

Behind a nearby bush she saw several little wolf cubs. Most of them were watching their parents with interest as they saw off the three men, but one of the young wolves was looking straight at her as she zoomed away on the back of the snowmobile. "That must be Willow!" thought Maya. "I wish I could take her with me, but it's best for her to be here with her family." She waved, and Willow wagged her tail and watched until the hillside dipped sharply downwards and they were lost from sight.

Within ten minutes they had arrived at the town of Bratska. It was wonderful to see people going about their normal lives, mostly making their way home as the time drew towards midnight. Twinkling streetlights reflected off the snowy roofs, which felt a million miles away from the gloomy cell they had been imprisoned in just a few hours earlier.

PLATFORM OF PERIL

"We still need to be careful," Maya's dad warned. "Dr Stoker has spent a lot of money in this area and has powerful friends here. We won't be safe until we're on the plane back to St Petersburg."

He went with Tao to return the rented snowmobiles, while Maya's mum bought train tickets to nearby Krasnoya, the closest airport. Maya felt almost sick with tension as they boarded the train and then waited for it to depart. The escapees spoke very little, everyone watching nervously to see if Dr Stoker would try anything else to bar their progress. The scheduled time of departure came and went, and their train remained stubbornly rooted in place.

"What's happening?" Maya asked her parents. "Why aren't we moving?"

"Trains are held up all the time, it may be nothing to worry about," her father reassured her – but the look he exchanged with Maya's mum revealed they were just as concerned by the delay as she was.

Maya had her face pressed against the window, looking at the small station house for any signs of activity. Seeing movement at the doorway, she felt a momentary surge of hope that it would be a railway official coming to send the train on its way. These hopes were dashed in the cruellest way possible as the dreaded figure of Ms Kotka strode out onto the long, windswept platform of the station, followed by six or seven of the Taymira guards in their grey uniforms. The teacher's words were inaudible through the glass but Maya watched her quick, sharp gestures as she split the guards into pairs and gave them each a section of the train to search.

Maya pulled away from the window to avoid being seen and warned the others. Looking around in desperation, they saw there were no possible places of concealment nearby. Tao pointed towards the door leading on to the next carriage, and as a group they filed through it as quickly and quietly as they could. The next compartment was just the same: plain rows of seats that offered no prospect of a hiding place. They continued, making their way towards the rear of the train.

Eventually they came to the final carriage, which was clearly intended for the storage of luggage. With two rows of wide shelving on either side of the aisle, it seemed the best of their limited options. Without words, her parents waved the children into the spaces under the lowest shelf, moving a few suitcases to provide more cover and then crawling in themselves. Maya found herself wedged in between her father and Jessie, with her friend's knees pressing painfully into her back. She felt Jessie tremble, her usual optimism and bravery tested to the limit by their desperate situation. Reaching back she located and squeezed Jessie's hand.

"We'll be okay," she whispered hopefully, feeling a sharp pang of guilt over the way her friends had been drawn into danger because of her.

They listened to the guards making their way towards them through the train. After a minute or two, the door of the luggage carriage flew open with a crash and Maya saw two pairs of black boots advancing down the aisle. The men halted not far from where she lay, and began moving cases on the higher shelves, occasionally whispering comments to each other too quietly for Maya to hear.

"This is it," she thought desperately. "I bet they're armed to the teeth, and in this cramped space we've haven't a hope of getting away. They'll find us – and what then? We'll be dragged back to Taymira to be Stoker's guinea pigs for ever. He'll probably make up some nonsense about us being involved in a fatal hopscotch accident or something, so nobody comes looking! All I can do is beg him to let Jessie and Ella go; he doesn't really need them, he only wants me so he can force my parents to do his dirty work. I bet he won't release them though – they know too much about his evil school."

Holding her breath to avoid making the slightest sound, she peered around her in the shadows to make out her parents' faces. Would she ever see them again after tonight, or would Stoker separate them to avoid any repeat of their escape? "It's crazy, but I don't regret coming here," she realised. "I might be in for a lifetime of imprisonment and cruel experiments, but at least I know my parents are still alive. Whatever Stoker does to me, I'll never stop trying to rescue them - never!"

Just at that moment, Maya caught a couple of words exchanged by the guards as they methodically worked their way through the baggage racks, and it seemed to cast a faint ray of light on her situation.

"… then we'll be legends, yeah?"

Hearing these words, Maya began to scramble out of her hiding place. Her father grabbed her arm, mouthing, "No! I'll deal with them," but Maya replied, "I've got this," and clambered over the cases to stand blinking in the bright light of the carriage before the guards.

The two men were none other than Snake and Vladders, the former of whom had adopted his familiar kung fu stance the moment he saw movement amongst the luggage, and remained frozen in that position, his face a picture of amazement. For a second nobody moved, until Snake broke the silence, exclaiming, "Maya! What the 'ell are you doing here? We're looking for dangerous criminals who broke into the lab and stole valuable top-secret science stuff – this ain't no place for a kid! That's why they sent me and Vladders, yeah? Coz we live for danger."

"Snake, you're a lovely guy – a legend, in fact – but you can be a plank-headed imbecile sometimes. Don't you see? *We* are the 'dangerous criminals' you've been sent to find: me and my friends, and my parents."

Snake gave a snort of incredulous laughter. "You? No offence Maya, but you're a little girl, yeah? You ain't dangerous, not to a top security mastermind like me. My uncle's got a lot on his plate, saving the world with science and all that, he wouldn't waste the time of his top advisors (like me) by sending us chasing after a bunch of kids. Don't worry though, your teacher's back there on the platform. I'll give her a shout and she'll look after you while we find those dodgy characters I told you about."

With these words the young man turned to open the window and call Ms Kotka, but Maya darted in front of him and grabbed the front of his jacket with both hands, making a last desperate plea. "Snake, please, listen to me!" she half shouted, half sobbed at the perplexed guard. "Your uncle isn't saving the world, he's an evil thug who only cares about finding fame and fortune for himself! He does sick experiments on children, and he'll stop at nothing to get what he wants: kidnapping, imprisonment, maybe even murder. Haven't you ever wondered why you see so many children being taken to the lab? You must have noticed them, on those monitors of yours."

"Well, yeah... but they go there to help... it's an honour to help a great scientist like Uncle Lesley."

"Haven't you noticed how most of them never come back?"

"Well, I haven't really thought about it," replied Snake, clearly taken aback by Maya's outburst. "Sometimes they come back: what about that Lola kid, she came back, yeah?"

"Yeah – after your uncle had driven her to the edge of madness with his cruel treatment. And then what? He decides she isn't fit to be in school anymore and turns her into an unpaid servant."

"She seems happy enough…"

"That's because she's never known any other life – she's been Stoker's lab rat since she was virtually a baby!" Pausing for breath, Maya continued in a gentler tone, "Look, I know you don't want to hear anything bad about your uncle… but I think deep down you must realise that something isn't quite right at Taymira. All I ask is that you let us go on our way – just go and tell Ms Kotka there's nobody on this carriage, and you'll never see us again."

Maya watched as a variety of feelings worked their way slowly across Snake's face – denial, then anger, then uncertainty. "Listen Maya," he said at length, "I get you, yeah? You want to go home. But think about me and Vladders: if we turn you in, we'll be heroes back at the school. Uncle Lesley will tell my Mum I've done a great job, and she'll be – you know – proud or whatever. Yeah?"

Here he glanced at his Russian friend for support, but Vladders gave an almost imperceptible shake of his otherwise expressionless features. Without the backing of his comrade, Maya sensed that Snake's resolve might instantly crumble, so she pressed her advantage.

"Think about it, Snake, you told me when we first met that you were dangerous. You don't play by the rules, you're a renegade, an outlaw… you're Hampshire's best rapper! Are you going to go along with the system, and be controlled by Dr Stoker? Or are you going to go your own way, take a stand, save a bunch of innocent children and become the ultimate legend?"

Her words clearly hit home, and the young man's face lit up. "Ultimate legend?" he repeated. "Well, when you put it like that, it does kind of sound like me… okay, Vladders – I've decided: we're going to go back out there and say this carriage is empty, yeah? Coz that's just the way we roll."

This drew a brief nod and a wink from his colleague.

"Maya – best of luck to you and your friends, yeah? I'm actually coming back to England in a few weeks, probably gonna lay down some tracks. You can come along to my first arena tour when I've made it big."

"Of course - let me just ask one more thing," Maya asked as the guards turned to go. "When you leave Taymira, please see if you can take Lola with you. I know all the children there are having a bad time, but nobody should have to bear what she has."

"I'll do what I can, kiddo," Snake replied over his shoulder, and the two young men hurried down the aisle and out onto the platform.

Peeping through the window, Maya saw them report to Ms Kotka who threw her hands up in frustration and stomped back towards the station house. After a couple more nervous minutes, the train finally started to move, quickly gathering speed and leaving Taymira far behind.

HOME

Only when the train was safely on its way could Maya start to relax. The others clambered out of their hiding place and congratulated her on her handling of the guards, and she got a chance to explain how she had recognised Willow's mother amongst the wolves who had saved them from being recaptured. "She knew it was us, and that we had rescued her daughter. How lucky they were close by and were ready to return the favour!"

To Maya's great relief they got to Krasnoya and boarded their plane without any trouble. "I think Dr Stoker was too busy trying to get back to his so-called school with some of his trousers left to worry about us!" said Jessie with a smile as they soared towards St Petersburg. There they took their leave of Tao and Adelina, who were catching a flight to their home town of Nummela in Finland. Tao had found some distant cousins who were happy to look after them and give them a place to stay.

"Maya, I am so grateful to all of you for helping us to escape from Taymira," Adelina said as they hugged each other goodbye.

"We're grateful to you too!" replied Maya. "You were one of the only friendly faces we saw in all our time at the school. We would have been quite miserable without you."

"You must come and visit us in England soon!" added Ella. "Message us as soon as you are settled in to your new home so we know you're OK."

After they had seen their two new friends safely onto their plane, they had to wait a few minutes for the next flight to London. Maya's parents made some phone calls, and her mum explained that they had spoken to some good people they knew in Moscow and told them everything that had happened in Siberia. "It won't be easy," she said, "but we won't rest until that school has been shut down and all the children returned home."

Once they were in the air once more on the final part of their journey home, Maya felt like pinching herself to make sure she wasn't dreaming. Was it really just four days ago she had been flying out towards the Taymira Academy, believing herself to be an orphan who would never see her family again?

Now here she was once more, with Jessie and Ella next to her just like before – but this time instead of Ms Kotka's severe scowl she saw her parents smiling back at her from across the aisle, as they discussed how to bring Dr Stoker to justice.

A few weeks later Maya was back at the bottom of Aunt Jane's garden, feeding tiny leaves to Woody. After a joyful reunion, it had been decided that Maya and her parents should stay there until they had time to find a new home. It was a perfect peaceful autumn day, disturbed only by the occasional chirping of a blackbird and the lazy buzz of a hedge trimmer from the garden next door. Maya's Mum had given her a picnic basket to eat her lunch outside, although she had made little progress with it. Woody proved to be an excellent listener, and Maya had been regaling him with the full story of her time in Siberia.

"... and you'll never guess what," she concluded. "It turns out Snake really was a legend, just like he always told us. Vladders found Lola's passport buried under some paperwork in Professor De Molle's office, and when Snake left Taymira to come home he smuggled Lola out with him. Her passport had the name of the town where she was born, and a lovely children's charity is arranging for her to be taken back there and looked after. Meanwhile, there's no point scaly old Ms Kotka coming looking for Katia to drag her back to that awful school – as soon as we left for Russia, Katia disappeared. She left a note saying she had a great-grandmother living in Paris, and she was going off to find her. So with those two, plus Adelina and Tao, and of course the three of us, at least that's seven children who won't be used as guinea pigs anymore!"

"Mum and Dad are doing their best to get the school closed down, and it seems like they're finally making some progress; apparently the Russian police showed up at Taymira yesterday to ask some questions but Stoker was nowhere to be found. I can't tell you what it's like to have parents again… last night Dad told me off for not brushing my teeth and I just started crying; not because I was sad, but just because I've missed all those little things… I know it's silly, but do you know what I mean?"

Woody waved an antenna, as if he knew exactly what she meant and thought it wasn't silly at all. Just then Aunt Jane showed Ella into the garden, and she skipped down to where Maya was sitting with her little pile of leaves. Not for the first time, they were soon talking about Taymira and all the strange people they had met on their travels.

"Do you remember how excited we were on the way out?" asked Ella. "I knew it was going to be an amazing trip, but I didn't expect to be thrown in a dungeon, chased by a helicopter or rescued by wolves! I wonder if we'll ever have an experience like that again in our whole lives, even if we live to be a hundred and thirty-nine!"

"Yes, I wonder..." Maya replied.

She noticed that the noise from next door's garden had subsided, leaving an expectant silence. Feeling a strange sense of unease, Maya put a finger to her lips and looked around, her eyes and ears seeking anything out of the ordinary. For a moment all was still, until the hedgerow in front of them suddenly parted and a strange figure crashed through it into their garden, reaching towards them with a strangled snarl of unmistakable malice.

THE KNOCKOUT BLOW

Maya scrambled to her feet and looked at the intruder in amazement. Despite the grubby clothes and the twigs and leaves sticking out of his ruffled hair, there was no mistaking the unpleasant form of Dr Stoker. He had a wild, dangerous glint in his eye and looked as if he had not slept for days – a far cry from the smooth, professional veneer the girls were used to seeing. Holding a hedge trimmer in one hand, he grabbed Ella roughly with the other and advanced towards Maya.

"So, young lady," he growled, "it seems I've got the better of you at last! You're going to come along quietly with me, or else Miss Kelley here is going to have a little trim, hah hah!"

Laughing manically, he pressed a button on the hedge trimmer, making its blades buzz menacingly. "Don't worry, you won't be harmed, and you can come back home to Mummy and Daddy – as soon as they make a statement that they made up all the nasty things they've been saying about my wonderful school and glorious laboratory. Once the police stop poking around and my reputation is restored, they can have you back – not before!"

"Your reputation?" Maya replied in disbelief. "You lock up children and animals and do dangerous experiments on them… you're a liar, a kidnapper, a talentless loser who tries to take credit for other people's work, and probably a murderer too! What kind of a reputation do you deserve?"

"Talentless?" Stoker replied, seeming to take great offence at this word rather than the many worse things Maya had called him. "That's what they said about me at school – that's what my mother called me too – but I showed them! I showed them all! Someday my name will be mentioned in the same breath as Albert Einstein or Isaac Newton… the great Lesley Stoker, finest mind of his generation."

Despite the danger they were facing, Maya couldn't suppress a derisive snort. "You haven't got the finest mind in this garden, let alone anywhere else, and your name will only be mentioned in the same breath as the other crooks you find yourself in prison with."

"That's enough!" Stoker shouted. "I don't have to listen to you... just come with me right now, and nobody will get hurt."

With these words he jabbed the hedge trimmer threateningly towards Ella, who was struggling to release herself from his grasp. Maya looked around for something to use as a weapon but there was nothing to hand except the remains of her picnic, which lay on the grass in front of her along with her basket. A vague idea seemed to nudge the back of her mind as she looked at the food and drink that was left: a banana, a slice of lemon cake and a glass of chocolate milk. "How is any of that helpful?" Maya thought, desperately racking her brain. "Does he love lemon cake? No, there was no nice food at Taymira so I assume not... come on Maya, think!"

Suddenly, the thought at the back of her mind leapt forward to the front and presented her with a plan. "OK, I'll come with you, just let Ella go," she told Dr Stoker. "My head is spinning though, I've got to have a drink."

She put her hand to her forehead as if on the verge of collapse, and reached down to grab her glass. Taking a quick sip she advanced towards Stoker, who pushed Ella away and reached out to grab Maya instead, saying, "You've made the right decision for once Maya – now hurry!"

As soon as Ella was out of range of the doctor's improvised weapon, Maya lunged forward and hurled her chocolate milk in his face. It hit its target with a satisfying splosh, drenching Stoker's features in brown liquid and covering his glasses, which he reached up to wipe frantically.

"Run, Maya!" shouted Ella, sprinting away down the garden, but Stoker's blindly flailing hands had succeeded in grabbing Maya's wrist and were holding her tight.

"Stupid child!" the principal snarled. "Did you think the mighty Dr Lesley Stoker could be stopped so easily? You're not dealing with one of your little friends in the playground here, but one of the world's greatest thinkers..."

Stoker's voice trailed off at the end of this little speech, as if his throat was closing up around his words. Releasing both the hedge trimmer and Maya, he put first one hand to his neck, then the other, before doubling over in obvious pain.

"Maya!" he wheezed. "What was in that drink?"

"Can't you tell? As one of the world's greatest thinkers, I would have thought you might be able to detect the main ingredients; there's chocolate of course, and let me see, what's the other thing? Oh yes, it's the very thing you're allergic to: milk!"

Fighting for breath, with his hands on his knees, Stoker took a moment to reply, "You haven't beaten me... I just need a minute..."

With no way of knowing whether this was true or not, Maya was taking no chances. Grabbing her picnic basket she swung it in the air and then directed it into the doctor's face, connecting with a loud crunch. Stoker dropped to the floor in a heap and lay there in a daze, quietly mumbling, "I'm still the best... you haven't beaten me... I'm the greatest," even as Maya tied his hands with garden twine and then ran to get her parents.

~o~

"How on earth did you know he would be allergic?" asked Maya's mum, after the police had collected Dr Stoker and taken him away.

"I didn't know for sure," Maya explained. "I remembered he drank black coffee, and then we saw he had been reading a document about dairy allergies. Knowing how selfish he is, I thought that would probably only be because he suffered from them himself."

"Well, you were very brave to stand up to him, just like you did back in Siberia. Just promise me that will be the end of your adventures – I want you to have a normal, quiet life from now on."

"Sure, no more excitement, I promise," Maya replied, crossing her fingers behind her back. Somehow she had the feeling that adventure would always be just around the corner – if she knew where to look.

THE END

THANK YOU for reading Lost Snowflakes. If you enjoyed Maya's adventures, it would mean a lot to me if you could take a moment to leave a book review on Amazon, GoodReads or social media. For an independent author like me, this can be crucial in helping other readers decide if Lost Snowflakes belongs on their shelf.

Until the next time - happy reading!

~Linton~

For more information about Maya Madison and her adventures…

www.LintonDarling.com
@LintonDarling

Made in the USA
Coppell, TX
18 November 2020